DELIVERING THE BABY

"Well," said Felicity, "I hope you've figured out a plan. We can't just go up to their door and say 'Hello, Malcolm. Here's a baby for you.' "

Sara realized there was some truth in what Felicity said.

After a moment's pause, as the baby gurgled with pleasure, Sara's eyes lit up with a brilliant idea. "I know, Felicity! You could bring Abigail or Malcolm down to the pond, and then I could float the baby over to you in its basket, just like Moses in the bulrushes!"

Felicity looked at her with alarm. "Don't be ridiculous, Sara, he might drown!"

Sara nodded, her face falling. Then a twinkle came to her eyes. "Well then, why don't we just leave him on their doorstep?"

Felicity bit her bottom lip. "Under the cover of darkness!" she added, their minds in harmony.

"With a note!" finished Sara triumphantly, barely able to contain her joy. They grinned conspiratorially and shook hands on it.

Also available in the Road to Avonlea series from Bantam Skylark Books

Malcolm and the Baby

Storybook written by
Heather Conkie

Based on the Sullivan Films Production
adapted from the novels of

Lucy Maud Montgomery

A BANTAM SKYLARK BOOK
NEW YORK · TORONTO · LONDON · SYDNEY · AUCKLAND

Based on the Sullivan Films Production produced by Sullivan Films Inc. in association with CBC and the Disney Channel with the participation of Telefilm Canada adapted from Lucy Maud Montgomery's novels.

Teleplay written by Heather Conkie
Copyright © 1989 by Sullivan Films Distribution, Inc.

*This edition contains the complete text
of the original edition.*
NOT ONE WORD HAS BEEN OMITTED.

RL 6, 008-012

MALCOLM AND THE BABY

*A Bantam Skylark Book / published by arrangement with
HarperCollins Publishers Ltd.*

PRINTING HISTORY
HarperCollins edition published 1991
Bantam edition / November 1992

ROAD TO AVONLEA is the trademark of Sullivan Films Inc.

*Skylark Books is a registered trademark of Bantam Books,
a division of Bantam Doubleday Dell Publishing Group, Inc.
Registered in U.S. Patent and Trademark Office and elsewhere.*

ISBN 0-553-48034-0

PRINTED IN THE UNITED STATES OF AMERICA

OPM   0 9 8 7 6 5 4 3 2 1

Malcolm and the Baby

Chapter One

"I can't wait to see Aunt Abigail and Malcolm," said Sara Stanley, her blue eyes shining as she walked along the main street of Avonlea towards Lawson's general store with her Aunt Hetty and cousin Felicity.

"Imagine, a honeymoon in Boston," thirteen-year-old Felicity sighed. "Isn't that just *so* romantic?"

The brisk winds of autumn whisked around them, reddening their cheeks. The trees surrounding Avonlea were at the peak of their glory, with their crimson reds and golds glowing like fire among the stately pines.

This was Sara Stanley's first autumn in the little village on Prince Edward Island. She had loved the spring and she had revelled in the summer, but now her loyalties to those two seasons were completely torn. Never in all her travels from her home in Montreal had she seen such a flamboyant display of nature. She felt sure that fall would always be her favorite season in Avonlea.

Hetty King was not one to dawdle, and the two girls literally had to run to keep up with her. She strode along with purpose, her thin back erect, her empty wicker shopping basket primly over one arm, as if she were on an important mission that she and only she could accomplish.

"A honeymoon in Boston," she sniffed disapprovingly. "A dreadful distance, if you ask me. I don't see why they couldn't have stayed at the White Sands."

Romantic talk made Hetty uncomfortable. She herself had neither the time nor the inclination for such notions, and furthermore, she believed it quite unsuitable to encourage in others.

Hetty was not at all sure that the union of Abigail Ward and Malcolm MacEwan had been a good idea in the first place. She wondered how Janet King's spinster sister could possibly adjust to married life after so many years of calm self-sufficiency and freedom. She shook her head at the prospect. It was all very well that Mr. MacEwan had been Abigail's beau seven years ago, but a lot of water had passed under the bridge since he had disappeared out of her life. Goodness knows he had come back rich, but a mining camp in the Yukon was no place to learn good manners. The man was a barbarian as far as she could see. She feared the marriage was doomed to failure.

Twelve-year-old Sara had no such misgivings. In the months since she had arrived in Avonlea to stay with her Aunt Hetty and Aunt Olivia, she could remember many things that had given her pleasure. But of all her experiences, none had given her more delight than playing matchmaker for Abigail and Malcolm. No memory was so vivid as Aunt Abigail's frantic fit of despair when Sara and Felicity had reported the news that Malcolm MacEwan was preparing to return to the wilds of the Yukon, inconsolable after she broke their engagement. She would never forget the moment when prim and proper Abigail took the reins of the King buggy and, bonnet and hair flying, gave chase to the stagecoach that bore Malcolm MacEwan to the train station.

Sara took Felicity's arm conspiratorially and grinned up at her pretty older cousin with great self-satisfaction. Both girls glowed in the knowledge that they were fully responsible for their aunt and new uncle's happiness.

"And none of it would have happened without us, Felicity," Sara said triumphantly. "Malcolm MacEwan would be back in the Yukon by now."

"And Aunt Abigail would still be..." Felicity paused, "an old maid." She pronounced the words as though it were a mortal illness.

"Hmmph," snorted Hetty, a note of defensiveness entering her voice. "There are worse things to be, I'm sure, Felicity King." She was unmarried and proud of it. Her position as the eldest of the King tribe and the respected schoolmistress of Avonlea gave her a feeling of great satisfaction, as great, in its own way, as that of marriage. "In any case, you children have no business poking your noses into adult affairs."

"We were not poking our noses, Aunt Hetty," insisted Sara.

"We were simply making sure that Cupid's arrow found its mark," Felicity agreed smugly.

"Cupid's arrow, my auntie," huffed Hetty. She grabbed at her sensible hat as a particularly strong gust sent eddies of leaves swirling around the baskets of apples on the porch of the general store.

Just as they approached its steps, a billowing Mrs. Rachel Lynde appeared around the corner of the building. The minute the two women spotted one another, they stiffened.

"Look what the wind blew in," Hetty King was heard to mutter under her breath, and Sara looked at her aunt in surprise.

Rachel Lynde drew herself up to her full, imperious height, which, including her wildly beribboned and feathered black hat, was quite considerable. She possessively clasped her basket of sewing, as if the wind would grab it away from her at any moment, and gave Hetty a steady, unblinking glare. Sara could see a hint of a challenge in that look, and she watched her Aunt Hetty's face for its reaction.

Hetty King and Rachel Lynde were mortal enemies. They had not spoken to each other since the day that Rachel Lynde had allegedly stolen Hetty's beau, Romney Penhallow, thirty years ago. Sara could hardly fathom that something that had occurred in grade seven could have such far-reaching consequences, but Hetty was not one to forget an injustice. In fact, the one and only thing she and Rachel Lynde had in common was their stubbornness.

Hetty did not flinch as she matched Rachel's cold stare with a steely gaze of her own. Then, raising her nose in the air like a ship's beacon, she crossed to the other side of the road, directing Sara and Felicity to follow. Rachel watched her go and then sailed into the general store.

"What a hat!" Hetty humphed. "Who does she think she is, the Queen of England?"

The two girls hid their smiles, but Sara couldn't help saying, "Aunt Hetty, I thought we were going into the general store!"

"If that Rachel Lynde is in there, I'll do my business in the post office first." Hetty shivered in disgust. "I can't abide that woman. Never could."

Sara and Felicity shared a glance, rolling their eyes. Hetty turned to them, almost catching them in the act. Sara looked up at her with wide-eyed innocence as her aunt maternally straightened her scarf and tam.

"Now, you two," Hetty instructed, "mind you don't outstay your welcome with Malcolm and Abigail. Be back here in one hour, and no longer. I'll need you to help me carry the supplies home."

"We promise," said Sara, impatient to be off.

"Mm-hmm," said Hetty skeptically, rearranging Sara's blonde curls.

"Two lovebirds wouldn't want to be disturbed for long anyhow!" said Felicity with a giggle.

Sara grinned and broke away from her Aunt Hetty. "Race you!" she called to Felicity and ran off down the street in the wind, the crimson leaves scattering about her laced leather boots. Felicity waved to Aunt Hetty and took off after Sara in a most unladylike fashion.

Not like Felicity at all, Hetty thought. Perhaps Sara is rubbing off on her a bit. It certainly wouldn't hurt. She smiled and proceeded on her way to the post office.

Felicity caught up with Sara, and the two girls ran past the picket fence of Mrs. Biggins' boarding house, through the sudden, cool dimness of the covered bridge and out once again into the dazzling brightness of the woods. Sara delighted in the feel of the wind on her cheeks, and the faint smell of sea salt it carried with it. It made her feel that she could run forever. By the time they had reached the outskirts of Avonlea, they were both out of breath from running and giggling. They set off at once across the field, golden with autumn light, to Aunt Abigail's—and now Uncle Malcolm's—house.

Chapter Two

Abigail MacEwan surveyed her tiny parlor with dismay. All around her was a confusion of boxes and cartons, knick-knacks and wedding gifts, packing cases and straw. She ran her slim fingers through her auburn hair, her lower lip quivering. She was on the verge of tears. This was intolerable. She hated a mess. She couldn't help it. It was ingrained in her very bones.

All her life had been spent tidying. She had cooked and cleaned and cared for her dear mother when she was sick, and after she had passed on, her father, the tyrannical Reverend Ward, had, with unspoken expectations, ordained it her duty to keep house and care for him until the end of his earthly days. Abigail couldn't help but feel a tinge of jealousy towards her sister, Janet. She had married Alec King before their mother took sick, and since she was soon raising a family of her own, she had had very little time to help Abigail out, much as she had wanted to do so.

Finding herself blissfully alone after her father had died, Abigail had continued to clean for herself, and herself only. By that time, it had become a way of life, a way to feel that things were as they should be—organized and controlled. Tidy. She was known for her housekeeping. Her little parlor was always spic and span, everything in its place, its quiet unbroken save for the ticking of her grandfather's clock. That is, until Malcolm MacEwan had arrived back in Avonlea.

She sat back on her heels, dropping the silver tea service she had been unwrapping back into its crate. Everything has changed, she thought with a sudden, unbidden surge of remorse, filled with the memory of how simple life used to be. She shook her head sharply, angry with herself. How could she possibly feel such a wave of sadness when she had never been happier in her life?

She picked out the beautifully graceful teapot from the crate once again and admired it, running her fingers appreciatively over its carvings. She looked around the room for an available surface to put it on, then headed towards a small table as yet unencumbered with unpacked wedding gifts.

Malcolm was so generous. He would have bought her literally anything her heart desired in Boston, if she had let him. As it was, it seemed as if the entire contents of all Boston's many stores were right at this moment in her parlor. As she crossed the room she smiled gently, thinking of her new husband, and then promptly tripped over a pair of his boots that he had carelessly left lying right in the middle of the floor. The smile disappeared. She slammed the teapot onto the table, then picked up the boots and carried them to the hallway where they belonged.

Suddenly, she heard the sound of an approaching buggy. Looking expectantly through the dainty lace curtains on her front door, Abigail saw the buggy pull up outside. Malcolm MacEwan jumped gracefully from the front seat. She pulled the curtain aside, and her face fell. Something was visible in the back of the buggy, but it was covered with a blanket. What could he be bringing home now? A red blush of annoyance started creeping up her cheeks. She watched as he gave the horse a pat and strode around to jump just as nimbly into the back of the buggy.

Abigail flicked the curtain back over the window with some irritation and dropped the boots in the hall. "Oh Malcolm!" She sighed with resignation, a crooked smile on her face, and walked back into the parlor.

She stared up at her father's portrait, hanging imperiously on the wall above the small fireplace, his implacably stern face looking down at her accusingly. She could almost hear him say as he had once done so long ago, "Abigail, that

MacEwan lad is not good enough for you. I forbid you to see him again, let alone marry him." She had obeyed him back then, and Malcolm had disappeared from Avonlea, only to return seven years later, having proven her father wrong.

Abigail screwed up a ball of packing paper with surprising fierceness and threw it into the fire that glowed in the hearth. She jumped imperceptibly as the front door slammed shut.

"Abby! Where are you?" shouted a melodious voice with a broad Scottish accent.

Abigail straightened her shoulders and said in a very controlled tone of voice, "I am in here, Malcolm!"

The fine figure of Malcolm MacEwan filled the tiny doorway of the parlor. Broad-shouldered, long-legged, he seemed to dwarf everything else in the room. He had dark hair, a well-tended mustache and the weathered face of a man who had mined in the outdoors for a good many years. What was most arresting about Malcolm MacEwan, however, were his eyes—blue-black eyes that sparkled with pure delight and love of life. Eyes that missed nothing, that had spotted gold where hundreds of other men had trod, unseeing, over it. Eyes that looked with unabashed love and fondness at his new wife, a woman he had kept in his heart for seven long years in a mining camp, a woman who had refused him not once, but twice in his lifetime. He never looked upon her without thanking his lucky stars that she had finally realized how much they truly needed one another.

"Abby," he said with the excitement of a young boy. "Sit yourself down. I have something to show you."

Abigail turned to him. "You have been to the Simpson auction, haven't you?" she asked.

Malcolm grinned. "Well I did have a wee look... and it's a good thing I did, too!"

Abigail tried very hard not to be taken in by his smile, not to lose track of all that she had planned to say to him when he returned.

"Malcolm, how could you possibly go to another auction? We don't need another thing!" Her voice rose with exasperation. "You must have bought every knick-knack and bric-a-brac in the city of Boston! There isn't a square inch left in my little house!"

Malcolm raised an eyebrow, his eyes twinkling. "I beg your pardon, Mrs. MacEwan. *Our* little house."

Abigail crossed her arms over her pure white lace blouse and sighed.

Malcolm held up a finger and, turning, dashed into the hall. He returned triumphantly, carrying an almost new, white wicker cradle.

"It's a beauty, isn't it Abby?" he asked, although he could already see that the proud unveiling of his new possession had not produced the desired result. "Don't you think?" he continued, wondering at his wife's reaction.

Abigail stared at the tiny cradle, her face crumpling, fighting back tears. "We don't need a cradle, Malcolm," she said, her voice barely above a whisper.

"Not just at this very moment, but you never know, do you?" Malcolm smiled slowly.

Abigail swallowed and said even more quietly, "We discussed this, Malcolm. I told you how I felt."

Chapter Three

Sara arrived slightly ahead of Felicity at Aunt Abigail's little white picket fence, and she waited, panting for breath, for her cousin to catch up with her. They smiled when they saw the buggy, glad to see that both Abigail and Malcolm were at home. Felicity loved Aunt Abigail, her mother's only sister, and Sara shared those feelings as well, even though she wasn't a blood relative. Both of them, however, had fallen heavily for Malcolm. They loved his laughter and his singing and the tales he wove about his mining days. He let them stay up late at night, in front of the fire, listening, much later than the grown-ups would normally allow.

They ran up the path, with its tidy borders of miniature rosebushes on either side. Some of the pink blossoms were still in bloom, and Sara bent and picked one to give to Abigail as a welcome home present.

"Sara, you don't give someone a gift of something that already belongs to them," Felicity said imperiously, fussing at her chestnut curls under her beret.

Sara looked skyward and picked another rose, just to spite Felicity. Even though they were getting along much better than they used to, there were still times when Sara couldn't help but wish that Felicity would stop trying to lord it over her. She realized this was just Felicity's way, however, and so attempted to bear it patiently.

They reached the front door, with its spotless, white lace curtains, and Sara was about to knock when they realized it was already open. In fact, they could hear Malcolm's voice as clear as day as it floated out towards them.

"Oh goodness, Abby! I don't want to hear any more of that nonsense about you being too old to have a baby. Why, just look at yourself! Too old indeed! You looked like a lass of twenty the day I married you!"

Felicity and Sara looked at each other, Sara's hand frozen in a knocking position, inches away from the door. Abigail's voice reached them faintly, but just loud enough that they could certainly make out the words, and understand that she was very upset.

"Well, I've added some gray hairs since, learning to live with the likes of you, Malcolm MacEwan."

Sara and Felicity exchanged glances and quietly entered the front hall.

Unaware that they had an audience, Abigail stood with tears in her eyes. Malcolm crossed the room in two strides to hug her, but Abigail was not to be comforted.

"It isn't nonsense. It's a plain fact. Oh please, Malcolm, let's not discuss it again. I could never in my life see myself having a baby. I'm past that. Besides, I don't think I'm the mothering kind."

"You didn't think you were the marrying kind

either," said Malcolm quietly, still with a twinkle in his eye.

"Well, maybe I'm not," said Abigail with a catch in her voice, her father's portrait glaring at Malcolm over her shoulder. "Perhaps we shouldn't have married in the first place. I don't seem to be making you very happy."

Sara felt increasingly uncomfortable standing silently in the little front hallway. She hadn't meant to eavesdrop deliberately. She suddenly could see the truth in Aunt Hetty's old adage that an eavesdropper hears naught but ill tidings. Some things were simply too private to overhear, and any sense of exhilaration she may have felt intitially had passed quickly, replaced by a feeling almost of shame. She glanced at Felicity, who was still listening avidly.

Malcolm's good humor was sounding slightly ruffled.

"That's not true. I am happy, blast it! I love you!"

Abigail faced him, her face red from trying not to cry as a million unfamiliar emotions stirred within her.

"You won't be happy until we have a child! Look at you! Going around to auctions! Buying cradles! Bringing the subject up every other waking minute! I just can't! I don't want to discuss it anymore!"

"Fine! Let's not!" retorted Malcolm in a rare tone of impatience.

In the hallway, even Felicity was beginning to share Sara's discomfort. Sara nudged her, and they tiptoed out the front door, closing it quietly behind them.

Abigail looked down at her hands. She was not used to her husband's new tone of voice, and it had hurt her feelings even more. "Now take the cradle out and put it in the shed," she said quietly.

Malcolm shifted uneasily, feeling awkward and incapable of comforting his wife.

"All right!" He paused and then tentatively patted her shoulder. "I'm sorry, Abby. I didn't mean to upset you." He picked up the cradle and slowly carried it towards the door that led to the kitchen.

"It's all right," replied a subdued Abigail.

"Although it doesn't seem to take much these days," Malcolm threw over his shoulder as he disappeared into the kitchen.

"Oooooh!" exclaimed Abigail and, frustrated and upset, she picked up another ball of packing paper and flung it after him.

Chapter Four

A despondent Sara and Felicity trudged down the red dirt road towards the village of Avonlea. Suddenly, the scarlet and gold leaves of the trees weren't quite as bright. The wind was not exhilarating any longer, but simply a nuisance that pulled at your clothes, tangled your hair and made your nose run.

"Poor Aunt Abigail." Felicity shook her head in disbelief. "Poor Malcolm."

"How can anyone fight when they've just returned from a honeymoon?" Sara asked, holding the two drooping pink roses in her hand.

"Wait until I tell Mother," said Felicity.

Sara turned on her fiercely. "Don't you dare tell, Felicity King! It's private!"

"I suppose you're right," Felicity said grudgingly. "Besides, it would never do to let Mother know we had been eavesdropping."

"Well, we didn't really mean to," said Sara. She kicked at a stone with her boot and watched as it ricocheted into the ditch. "Maybe Aunt Hetty was right," she said forlornly. "We should never have meddled with them."

"Perhaps it is all our fault for getting them

together in the first place," lamented Felicity.

"No! They belong together!" said Sara with sudden conviction. "We've got to do something!"

"I think we've done enough," said Felicity, not realizing how often she would think back to those prophetic words over the next few days.

Chapter Five

The general store was a cozy place on a cool, crisp autumn afternoon, especially around the old potbellied stove, to which several chairs were always drawn up. A day didn't pass that someone or other didn't take time to sit awhile, have a neighborly chat and get caught up on the news or the latest gossip. Sometimes the proprietor, Mr. Lawson, would hold court there with various gentlemen from the village, reading the newspaper, discussing the current politics, or, more important, talking in hushed tones about the latest race results in Summerside.

On this afternoon, however, Mrs. Lawson was having a comfortable cup of tea with two of the ladies of Avonlea. She sat reading the latest edition of the Avonlea *Chronicle* as Rachel Lynde sewed in the chair opposite to her, tucked

behind a mannequin showing off the latest shirtwaist style from Montreal. Mrs. Potts was also in
attendance, knitting a small sweater, her needles
clicking just as busily as her mind as she listened
for tidbits of gossip that she could instantly pass
on to anyone else who would listen.

"You don't mind me setting here for a spell,
do you, Elvira May?" asked Rachel conversation-
ally. "It's dreadful quiet at home."

"Not at all Rachel," replied Mrs. Lawson
pleasantly. "I'm getting quite used to these little
visits."

"When's Marilla due back, Rachel?" asked
Mrs. Potts, hungry for information as usual.

Rachel sighed. "Oh, Anne won't let her go
for a few weeks yet I daresay, Mrs. Potts. The
new baby's jaundiced." Rachel leaned forward
conspiratorially. "It was obvious from her letter
that Marilla is exhausted."

Mrs. Potts nodded wisely, her double chin dis-
appearing into the lace ruffle at her throat. "She
should know better than to look after a baby at
her age." She held out the tiny, white wool gar-
ment and looked at it with great appreciation. "I
hope I can finish this sweater in time to send it
with one of your letters, Rachel."

"Well believe me, there's no rush, Mrs. Potts,"

Rachel assured her. "I won't be sending one till next week. Not enough news to fill many letters."

Mrs. Lawson looked up from the obituary column in the newspaper, her brow furrowed with puzzlement. "It says here that another 'octogenarian' has just died. What is an octogenarian?"

Mrs. Potts looked up from her knitting. "Whatever they are, they must be awful sickly creatures, for you never hear tell of them but they're dying."

Goodness knows whether this conversation would ever have shed some light on the true meaning of the word "octogenarian," for the ladies' conversation was interrupted by the bell on the door of the general store ringing, signifying the entrance of a customer.

The habitually curious Rachel Lynde peered around the side of the mannequin to see who it might be. Her sewing dropped to her lap. "Oh good Lord! It's Hetty King! Don't let on I'm here!" Rachel sank deeper into her chair and made good use of the mannequin as a shield.

Hetty looked furtively around, making sure that Rachel Lynde had finished whatever shopping she had to finish and had safely left the premises. She relaxed somewhat when she saw Mrs. Lawson and Mrs. Potts by the potbellied stove. The rest of the store appeared to be empty. She was just about to call Mrs. Lawson away from her newspaper and cup of tea when Mr. Lawson appeared from the rear of the store.

"Afternoon Hetty," said the affable proprietor. "What can I do for you?"

"I have a list as long as my arm, Mr. Lawson," said Hetty, reaching into her coat pocket and taking out a neatly folded piece of paper. "Sara's suddenly developed an appetite. She's been eating me out of house and home lately."

Rachel scrunched further out of sight behind the shirtwaist and whispered to Mrs. Lawson and Mrs. Potts out of the side of her mouth, "Hetty King is so tight, the poor child probably doesn't get half of what she needs to grow on!"

The women hid their smiles and glanced towards Hetty, who, catching their look from the corner of her eye, wondered what on earth they could possibly find so amusing in the extremely dull Avonlea *Chronicle*.

While Hetty read out her list and Mr. Lawson fetched the necessary articles, a cart piled high with furniture pulled up in front of the general store. It was a rough-hewn sort of rig, badly in need of a paint job, and its immaculately dressed driver was in sharp contrast to its dilapidated state. The slender, well-groomed young man stepped down from his seat awkwardly, in a way that revealed his inexperience with buggies. He straightened his cravat, making sure that the diamond stickpin was safely in place, pulled down on the vest of his three-piece, navy-blue suit, squared his shoulders and strode purposefully up the steps of the general store.

The bell rang once again, and Mr. Lawson looked up from serving Hetty as the very dapper young gentleman entered the store.

"I'll be with you in a minute, Mr....uh..."

The young man was staring at Hetty's back with obvious recognition when he realized Mr. Lawson was waiting expectantly for him to introduce himself.

"Theodore Simpkin, barrister and solicitor," he said with a courtly little bow.

Hetty's shoulders stiffened when she heard the voice and the name, and she slowly turned around to face the young man, her face cold and set, with more than a little disdain apparent upon it.

"Oh. What a pleasure to see you again, Miss King," stammered Mr. Theodore Simpkin, trying his best to hide his true feelings about the woman who stood before him.

Hetty had no such pretensions. She despised the man and couldn't care less if he realized it.

"I'm sorry I can't say the same, Mr. Simpkin. Excuse me." She turned back to the counter and studied her list.

She had had the misfortune of dealing with Mr. Simpkin once before in a situation concerning watering rights for the animals on the King farm. The young, inexperienced fop of a lawyer had taken his job far too seriously, as far as she was concerned, and had only served to complicate matters.

Mr. Simpkin bore no love for Hetty King, either. The fiasco over the water rights had almost cost him his job. These blasted country people, he thought to himself with contempt. The less I have to do with them the better. Mr. Simpkin much preferred the cosmopolitan atmosphere he enjoyed in his office in downtown Charlottetown. Why did his superior constantly give him the cases that involved mingling with these peasants in their little backwater villages? He cleared his throat imperiously, demanding Mr. Lawson's attention.

Mr. Lawson looked at him over the top of his wire glasses and spoke pleasantly but with uncharacteristic coolness. "If you don't mind, sir, I'll finish waiting on Miss King here and I'll get back to you...."

Mr. Simpkin interrupted him self-importantly. "Mr. Lawson, I am here on vital business. I represent the estate of the late Robert and Jane Morris. I believe the deceased had an outstanding account with your establishment."

Hetty's face turned as white as chalk, and she slowly turned around to face the man. "You don't mean Jane Morris...the public school teacher from Markdale...is dead?"

Mr. Lawson shook his head in amazement. "Why, I can hardly believe it...!"

The group around the potbellied stove reacted in shock as well. Mrs. Lawson dropped the obituary column as if, merely by reading it, she had somehow been responsible for this piece of news. Mrs. Potts slapped the sides of her cheeks with her chubby hands. Rachel Lynde was rarely shocked by anything, but all the color drained from her face, and her mouth fell open.

Chapter Six

Outside, Felicity and Sara walked slowly down the street towards the general store, looking at the cart with vague interest.

"Somebody must be moving," remarked Sara.

"From the looks of it, they certainly don't have much to move. And did you ever see such a broken-down cart? It's an eyesore," pronounced Felicity. Alec and Janet King's eldest daughter was very house-proud, and was apt to look down her nose on anything that she felt to be below King family standards.

"We'd better go in and see if Aunt Hetty has finished her shopping," said Sara. "I just want to go home where I can feel my sorrow for Abigail and Malcolm in private."

"But how...when did this happen?" Hetty had recovered from her initial shock and wanted some straight, clear answers.

A disinterested Mr. Simpkin took out his note-book. "Last week. They passed on within a day of each other. Scarlet fever, so I'm told."

"Oh, how dreadful," murmured Hetty, and then, with a sharp intake of breath, another thought occurred to her. "They just had a baby. I know they did! What has happened to the baby?" Hetty asked, her voice distraught.

Mr. Simpkin was busy looking through his notebook for the appropriate page, and answered distractedly, "Yes, yes, there was...three months old...Robert Morris Junior. Ah yes, here it is!" he announced, jabbing at the page with his well-manicured finger. He had finally found what he was searching for and looked up at Mr. Lawson in some triumph, eager to have this distasteful bit of business over and done with.

The doorbell rang again as Sara and Felicity entered the store, and Mr. Simpkin turned and surveyed them with annoyance, as if they had interrupted him on purpose. He turned back impatiently to Mr. Lawson.

"Now, according to my calculations, the deceased owed your establishment fifty-four dollars and twenty-six cents."

Mrs. Lawson's eyes flew open and she fairly leapt out of her chair and marched over to the counter. "Fifty-four dollars and twenty-six cents! Really Edward!"

Mr. Lawson looked at his wife sheepishly. "I don't usually let it run that high, but they seemed such a nice young couple."

Felicity and Sara looked from one grown-up to another, wondering what in heaven's name everyone was talking about.

Mr. Simpkin had neither the intention nor the time to listen to a domestic squabble, and he cleared his throat once again.

"I have had a man load a good portion of the

contents of their house onto a cart, which I drove here at great personal inconvenience. I am sure you will agree that their collective value is more than enough to pay off their debt."

Hetty could barely fathom how the insensitive man could stand there talking about collective value and debt when there were other, much more important things to be considered.

"But what is being done about the baby, Mr. Simpkin?"

Sara's ears pricked up. "What baby, Aunt Hetty?"

Hetty turned to her in surprise, unaware that the girls were even there. "Hush, Sara." She turned back to Mr. Simpkin.

The young man was again reminded of his dislike for this imperious woman. Who did she think she was, to question him? Was it not the lawyers who were supposed to do the questioning? "The baby?" he drawled, and gazed at her from under hooded lids, eyebrows arched. He had seen the magistrate in Charlottetown look at a man on trial in just such a way, and it had impressed him as being properly intimidating. "It's in a neighbor's care at present," he replied with studied indifference. "But I am taking it to the orphanage on my return to Charlottetown tomorrow."

Hetty King was not intimidated. "Orphanage!"

She spat the word out as if it were almost too distasteful to say.

Sara's eyes filled with sympathy. "Oh, the poor thing!"

Hetty strode quietly towards Mr. Simpkin, her hands on her hips, looking far more intimidating than any Charlottetown magistrate.

"Now listen here, Mr. Simpkin, Jane Morris was put under my supervision as a student teacher when she first arrived on the Island four years ago, and we became very close. I know for a fact that she would never want her baby put in the hands of the likes of you, or any orphanage."

Mr. Simpkin looked down at the perfect shine on his shoes and took an infinitessimal step backwards.

Hetty looked him straight in the eye. "I will find someone to care for that child!" she announced.

Sara looked at Felicity, her eyes wide with amazement. Behind the mannequin, Rachel Lynde's mouth finally snapped shut with decision. She rose up, making herself suddenly quite visible, a vision of indignation and resentment.

"You'll find someone to take care of it?" she bellowed like an outraged bull. "No relative of mine is going to be looked after by you, Hetty King! That child is my flesh and blood!"

The effect of this announcement was immediate. Mrs. Potts and Mrs. Lawson exchanged glances of pure astonishment. Hetty swung around, flabbergasted that Rachel was even in the store.

"What?" said a bewildered Mrs. Lawson.

"That's certainly news to me, Rachel!" huffed Mrs. Potts.

Hetty recovered herself enough to speak.

"Well, if that isn't just like you, Rachel Lynde. Skulking around like a fox near a henhouse!"

Sara had heard her aunt sound as angry and upset only once before, when she had tangled with Sara's Nanny Louisa on that first horrible night in Avonlea. She had won then. Sara wondered how she would fare with Rachel Lynde.

Rachel ignored Hetty's insult. "Robert Morris was my late husband Thomas's cousin's nephew!" she said with controlled ire.

Hetty snorted with contempt. "Oh my! That's a close family connection, I must say!" she said facetiously, her voice heavy with sarcasm.

Mr. Simpkin was relieved to see a light at the end of his legal tunnel. Perhaps he wouldn't have to be troubled with the infant after all. Stepping forward, he said heartily, "Well, in that case, Mrs...." he paused as Rachel swept towards him, ignoring Hetty King entirely.

"Lynde...Mrs. Thomas Lynde," she said grandly, holding out her hand.

Hetty was not about to see things taken out of her hands quite so easily. She stepped between Rachel and Mr. Simpkin. "You had no interest in the baby while the Morrises were alive," she said to Rachel accusingly. "Why should you have anything to say about its welfare now?"

Rachel jutted her chin out arrogantly and glared back at Hetty. "Finding a home for that baby is my duty, and I will not shirk it. I wouldn't want poor Thomas to think I'd let down his relations."

Hetty shrugged her shoulders. "I'm sure poor Thomas is beyond caring now."

Rachel's mouth formed the shape of an "O," and a red stain started creeping unattractively up her neck. But before she could get a word out, Hetty turned to Mr. Simpkin and said, with exaggerated, schoolteacher diction, "The baby needs a home. Look no further. It is my duty and I shall take it."

"Aunt Hetty! You can't mean it!" Sara grabbed at her aunt's hand, not knowing whether to be ecstatic or extremely anxious.

"Uh...I'm afraid, in the eyes of the law, it is not that simple, ladies...." stuttered Mr. Simpkin, wishing he could be anywhere else but in this godforsaken store. He might have saved his breath, for neither woman seemed to have heard him, or cared to.

"Aunt Hetty!" insisted Sara, tugging at Hetty's hand.

Hetty pulled her hand from Sara's. "Don't interfere with grown-up affairs, Sara. Go outside immediately!"

Rachel advanced menacingly towards Hetty. "Over my dead body, you'll take this baby! I'll keep the infant myself before I let you have it, Hetty King."

"Aha! You're just plain jealous! That's what you are, Rachel Lynde!" hissed Hetty. "Sara, leave at once!"

Sara had no intention of leaving. Things were becoming much too interesting.

Rachel had advanced even closer to Hetty. "Jealous!" she spat out. "Of you? For what possible reason?"

All the venom that had been stored up for thirty years between the two women threatened to burst forth as they stood, eye to eye, glaring at one another.

"You've always had an insatiable desire to have what is mine," accused Hetty.

"I don't know what you are talking about, Hetty!" responded Rachel.

"Oh yes you do,' Rachel Lynde! You know exactly what I'm talking about! You stole Romney Penhallow's heart away from me in grade seven, because you couldn't stand the idea that I had something that you couldn't have!"

"Oh my goodness, ladies, let's not drag that old chestnut out again," said Mrs. Potts, rolling her eyes at Mrs. Lawson.

Rachel and Hetty stood with their hands on their hips, scowling at one another. Hetty spoke quietly but with great purpose. "Jane Morris was more my friend than your relative, that's for sure. And I won't have you stealing her baby away from me! Oh no." She shook her head. "This time, you can't have something that is rightfully mine!"

"Rightfully yours!" repeated Rachel, in wonder at the gall of the woman.

Now, Mrs. Lawson was a peace-loving individual. She was not given to public outbursts herself, and was embarrassed by them when they arose among others. Even though she wasn't the most intuitive of people, she suddenly felt things had gone a bit too far, and as proprietor of the store, she knew it was her duty to try to calm the situation.

"Rachel! Hetty!" she implored as she stepped

between the two women. "Please, let's just sit down and have a nice cup of tea..."

Neither Rachel nor Hetty had any intention of sitting down and having tea, nice or otherwise.

"You just stay out of this, Elvira," said Rachel bluntly, pushing her friend out of the way.

Sara and Felicity watched, their eyes agog.

"Oh!" said an astonished Mrs. Lawson, moved almost to tears by such treatment. Mrs. Potts clucked disapprovingly and put a comforting arm around her friend.

Mr. Lawson was compelled to step in. "Ladies! Please!"

A thoroughly bored and annoyed Mr. Simpkin cleared his throat loudly. He did not like the feeling that everyone had forgotten he was even in the room. "Ladies, ladies!" he said condescendingly, in a voice he was training to carry to the back of a courtroom. "The fact is, Miss King, that if Mrs. Lynde is the child's only next of kin, then she is its legal guardian."

Hetty responded by pushing Mr. Simpkin out of the way with surprising power. The poor man was caught off balance and ended up sitting in a bag of potatoes.

"You see! I was right!" crowed Rachel Lynde triumphantly.

"Well, if you think you can get away with it, you're mighty mistaken!" said a furious Hetty. Turning, she realized that Sara and Felicity were still in the store. "Sara! Felicity! For the last time. Wait outside!!"

This time Sara knew her aunt meant it. She grabbed Felicity's hand and dragged her out of the store. Rachel Lynde's strident voice rang in their ears as the bell rang and the door slammed behind them.

"I'd like to see you stop me, Hetty King!"

Chapter Seven

Mr. Simpkin finally succeeded in extricating himself from the bag of potatoes. With what dignity he had left, he brushed the dirt off his suit, highly annoyed. "I did not spend four years studying law to traipse all over this godforsaken countryside to settle a dispute over an orphan," he fumed.

"There is no dispute to settle!" Hetty snapped. "This woman is far too old to even consider raising the child!"

Rachel's mouth dropped. "Too old! How dare you!" This was simply too much. She picked up whatever her eye fell on first, which happened to be a fresh roll from a basket on the counter, and flung it at Hetty. Hetty saw it coming and ducked. Of course, as luck would have it, Mr. Simpkin took it square in the chest. Mrs. Potts screamed and took refuge behind the counter.

With a gleam in her eye, Hetty reached for a potato and threw it at Rachel. Rachel hid behind the mannequin, using it as a shield, and the potato bounced off and rolled away.

Mr. and Mrs. Lawson stood behind the counter, not believing what they were witnessing. "Rachel! Hetty! Stop this!" sputtered Mr. Lawson, ineffectually.

"You should be ashamed of yourselves," said a righteously innocent Mrs. Potts, peeking out from behind the counter.

An outraged Rachel peered over the shoulder of the mannequin. "Hetty King! You don't know the first thing about raising children!"

Hetty put down the potato she was about to fling, thinking that action somewhat incongruous with what she was about to say. "I am a teacher, Rachel!"

"Those who can, do. Those who can't, teach!" Rachel spat back, slowly emerging from behind her protective shield.

"I would be a better mother to that child than you, Rachel Lynde!" challenged Hetty.

Sara watched through the store window, her hands cupping her face, not wanting to miss anything.

"Don't, Sara," Felicity admonished. "Aunt Hetty will see you."

Sara shrugged and came away from the window. To tell the truth, she had overheard more in one day than she cared to in a whole lifetime. Even from the front steps of the general store, she was able to make out most of what was being said.

"If I may just interject!" That dreadful Mr. Simpkin was trying to be heard above the din.

Hetty replied, "Oh be quiet, you young windbag!" Sara had to smile. He should know better than to tangle with her aunt.

Suddenly, Sara heard a faint sound that was quite unlike the raucous voices coming from inside the general store.

"What was that?" she asked Felicity, who, bored with the argument, was ambling over towards the furniture-laden buggy.

"Aunt Hetty calling that lawyer a windbag," Felicity replied absently as she looked with curiosity at the odds and ends stacked upon one another in the cart.

Sara frowned with concentration. She could have sworn... "There! I heard it again!" she cried.

"How could you hear anything but Rachel Lynde and Aunt Hetty carrying on?" commented Felicity as her eyes roamed over the heap of furniture and household odds and ends.

"No, listen Felicity, really," insisted Sara. "It's like...crying or something." She got up from the steps of the general store and walked towards the buggy. There it was again. A tiny cry. This time, Felicity reacted, her hand stopping in midair as she reached out to touch a silk tassel on a faded chair cushion.

"Did you hear it?" asked Sara excitedly.

"Yes," replied Felicity quietly. "It sounded like...," she hardly dared to say what the noise had unmistakably resembled.

Sara lost no time. She ran to the back of the buggy. A pair of old chairs, their blue-green paint peeling, were stacked one upon another, and underneath their rails was a two-handled wicker laundry basket full of old blankets.

Once again they heard a small cry amongst all the other noise.

"It came from here!" Sara said excitedly. She

lifted a blanket from the top of the basket. Both girls sucked in their breath. There, staring up at them, tears running down its pudgy red cheeks, was a baby! A tiny baby! It had obviously just woken up and was not at all pleased with the circumstances it found itself in.

"It's a baby! A real baby!" Sara looked at it with pure delight.

"Of course it's a baby," said Felicity impatiently, rolling her eyes at Sara's statement of the obvious.

"Felicity! Don't you see?" enthused Sara, her mind skipping and hopping over all that she had seen and heard in the general store. "It's the baby! The one they're all fighting about! It has to be!"

Felicity nodded slowly. She hated to admit it, but Sara was probably correct in her assumption. The baby let out another healthy sob.

"Poor thing. Just think what its future holds, living with Rachel Lynde." Felicity shook her head at the very thought.

Sara's blue eyes clouded over with concern. "Or in an orphanage!" She knew only too well what it felt like to be bereft of one parent. What could it possibly be like to lose both of them?

A stab of memory shot through her as she stood looking down on this helpless little baby.

Her own mother had died when she was only three years old. She knew she was fortunate to have had a very privileged childhood, indulged by a wealthy father and spoiled by her wonderful Nanny Louisa, but though she loved them both intensely, from the bottom of her heart, there was always an empty spot in her life that could never be filled.

The thought of her dear father, at home in Montreal, battling a court case that she still didn't quite understand, brought tears to her eyes. How she missed him. She remembered how she had felt when she first arrived in Avonlea—unwanted, unloved, intimidated by her mother's eldest sister, Aunt Hetty. Things were certainly different now, and she wouldn't trade her Aunt Hetty or Aunt Olivia or the rest of her mother's family for anything or anyone, but she couldn't help thinking, as she looked down on this beautiful little creature, that she would do anything she could to prevent it from going somewhere where it was unloved.

"Sara, we've got to tell them," said Felicity, interrupting Sara's thoughts and bringing her back to earth with a bump.

"No," said Sara suddenly.

"What do you mean, no?" said Felicity. "Of course that's what we have to do!"

Hetty King had often accused Sara Stanley of acting before thinking, and this occasion would certainly have given her ample evidence in support of that opinion.

"We've got to take it!" said Sara decisively.

"Take it!" said a flabbergasted Felicity. "What are you talking about?"

At that very moment, a potato came flying out through one of the windows of the general store, sprinkling shards of glass all over the front porch.

Sara motioned to the store. "Do you want any of them to look after it? They're not fit to." She started to pull the basket out from under the rungs of the chairs. Felicity stood absolutely still with her mouth open, not quite believing what Sara was doing.

"Here, take a handle," said Sara, in a voice so full of certainty that Felicity automatically did as she was told.

"Sara!" she protested, even as she took the weight of the basket in two hands.

"C'mon! Hurry!" said Sara, and they started to make their way down the street in the direction of the blacksmith's.

Abner Jeffries, covered in dirt and sweat, chose that same moment to wander out of the shop. Avonlea's "Appointed Chief Constable," as he liked to call himself, felt quite responsible for the well-being of his village, and in the middle of a stretch and a yawn, his unbelieving eyes witnessed yet another potato winging its way out of a broken window of the general store. He prided himself on his swift reactions to all that might be amiss and was immediately and acutely aware of the raucous noise issuing from the same premises. He looked dumbfounded, then awkwardly searched for his official whistle. He found it and, racing towards the store, blew it several times. He ran right past Felicity and Sara, who walked with the basket, eyes straight ahead, whistling.

As he passed, they looked at each other, breathed a sigh of relief and hurried down the road, carrying their precious cargo.

Chapter Eight

Potatoes and rolls littered the floor of the general store. Mr. and Mrs. Lawson, Mrs. Potts and Mr. Simpkin had all taken cover behind the counter, peeking up from time to time to see if the coast was clear. Rachel and Hetty faced each other, nose to nose.

"As I live and breathe," Rachel said to Hetty between her teeth, "you have the nerve of a plough horse!"

"At least I don't have its figure!" Hetty said in triumph, knowing she had hit her mark.

She had indeed hit a nerve. An incensed Rachel completely lost her normal good sense and gave Hetty a resounding slap across the face.

Four pairs of eyes widened in horror from behind the counter.

For a moment, Hetty stood stunned, a red patch glowing on her cheek where Rachel's hand had connected with it. Even Rachel was dazed and aghast at what she had done. What ever would Marilla say?

Hetty's quiet fury looked for a vent and, almost instinctively, her hand went for a bowl of eggs that had previously escaped her attention. A small smile formed on her face as she felt the smooth oval surface of her weapon. Everyone held their breath.

Suddenly, the bell on the front door clanged noisily and Constable Jeffries charged into the store and blew his whistle. Mrs. Potts and Mr. and Mrs. Lawson stared at him from behind the counter. Mr. Simpkin rose slowly and stepped forward cautiously and imperiously.

Hetty stood frozen with her hand above her head, egg at the ready. She looked at Abner and then back at Rachel. The temptation was just too much to resist. She cracked the egg directly on Rachel's forehead and watched as the poor woman stood there, absolutely stunned, the yellow yolk and clear egg white dripping down her face.

"What is the meaning of this?" demanded Abner Jeffries. Hetty smiled with satisfaction and, completely ignoring the "Appointed Chief Constable," turned and walked out the door of the general store.

Rachel, in a state of shock and embarrassment, searched desperately for her handkerchief and then dabbed at her face, as Mrs. Potts fluttered about her, offering condolences.

Mr. and Mrs. Lawson, looking around at the state of their store, were not quite as sympathetic. Mr. Simpkin was walking towards Abner Jeffries, wondering what sort of poor excuse this was for a police constable, when he stepped on a potato, lost his footing and ended up ignominiously on the seat of his pants on the floor of the general store.

Chapter Nine

The late-afternoon sun streamed through the window of the hayloft in the King barn, particles of dust golden in its rays. The swallows wafted in and out the open window above Felicity and Sara's heads as they sat taking turns holding the baby in the soft, warm straw.

Sara looked down into the baby's tiny face with awe. She had never really seen one up close before.

Her older cousin was looking at her with great concern, a frown on her pretty face. "Are you sure, Sara? You heard Aunt Abigail!" Felicity was having a very difficult time reconciling herself to the plan that Sara had just revealed.

"She only said she didn't want to *have* a baby," explained Sara. "But this one is already here! Once she sees how beautiful he is, she won't be able to say no!"

From the moment that Sara had laid eyes on the baby, she knew he was the answer to Aunt Abigail and Uncle Malcolm's dreams.

"Maybe you're right," said Felicity, although her voice was still filled with doubt. "Mother says Aunt Abigail never knows what she wants until it's staring her right in the face."

"How could they not love him?" said Sara, as the baby clutched onto her little finger and tried to get it into his mouth. "He's so beautiful." She and Felicity shared a smile. "Just look at his little hands, his tiny fingernails. Everything is so perfect!"

The perfect baby let out an unearthly wail and Sara quickly handed him over to Felicity.

"Except he's starving," said the ever-practical Felicity, holding the baby expertly and substituting her finger for the bottle he longed to suck on. "We'll have to find some milk for him." Felicity had plenty of experience with babies. She often liked to brag that she had "brought up" her younger brother Felix and her little sister Cecily, a fact that her mother silently disputed.

"And we'll need some supplies," added Sara. "Blankets and nappies and—"

"I can get them," said Felicity.

Sara looked at her cousin with curiosity. "How?"

"I'll sneak them," said Felicity, matter-of-factly. "Mother will never notice they're gone. They've been up in the attic for ages."

Sara looked at Felicity with admiration. "Felicity. You amaze me. I didn't know you had it in you."

Felicity shrugged, pleased with the compliment but still full of apprehension. "Well, Sara Stanley," she said. "I guess we're in this together."

Chapter Ten

The chaos of the general store was far from the idyllic scene in the King barn. Mrs. Lawson sat in front of her potbellied stove in tears. A subdued Rachel sat as still as a statue as Mrs. Potts, still clucking her disapproval of such goings-on, attempted to wipe the remaining egg from her face. Mr. Simpkin stood to one side, as close to the doorway as he could get, surveying the damage. Abner paced back and forth, trying to look as official as he could, as Mr. Lawson swept up the remains of the rolls and potatoes, and, of course, the egg.

"I oughta charge you all with public mischief!" blustered Abner. "I never seen anything like it in all my life."

Mr. Simpkin yawned and felt it was time to remind everyone of the matters at hand.

"Mr. Lawson, I would appreciate it if we could settle the matter of the account. I do not have all day to waste."

"Well, I'd like to know who is going to settle my losses!" fumed Mr. Lawson, looking up from his dustbin, broom in hand.

Mr. Simpkin looked at the unfortunate Mrs. Lynde and tried hard to control a cruel smile that threatened to curl his lip.

"Mrs. Lynde, I shall have to look into your claim to the Morris baby. If all is well, I can draw up the appropriate papers and deliver the baby to you tomorrow."

Rachel's jaw dropped. For the first time, she realized that her temper might have got her into more trouble than she'd bargained for. "That soon?" she gasped.

She was about to explain to the young man that she couldn't possibly be ready to accept a child into her home on such short notice when the bell clanged again, and a girl of about sixteen rushed into the store. She had a ruddy complexion and dark, curly hair to her shoulders. She looked around the war-torn store with a bewildered expression on her face until her eyes fell on Theodore Simpkin.

"Mr. Simpkin?" she said timidly.

Mr. Simpkin rolled his eyes, a "what next?" expression on his face. "Yes, Miss Purdy?"

"Ma wants to know if you already took the Morris baby to the orphanage?" The girl spoke rapidly and breathlessly, as if she had run a long way.

"Of course not," said an annoyed Mr. Simpkin.

"Does it look like I've already left for Charlottetown? What is wrong with you country people? I told her I'd pick the baby up tomorrow."

"Well then, where is it?" insisted Margie Purdy.

Everyone in the store stopped what they were doing. Even Mrs. Lawson ceased sobbing long enough to listen.

Slowly, it dawned on Theodore Simpkin what this farm girl was trying to say to him. "I beg your pardon?" he asked slowly and quietly. "I left your mother in charge of that baby! Are you trying to tell me that she's lost it?"

"No sir! At least, I knew where he was. Ya see, Ma was busy with my little brothers so she made me look after him, and lord if he didn't scream to high heaven. Didn't matter what I did with him. I figured he'd be a whole lot happier on his own front porch so I took him next door to the Morris house."

"There was no baby on the Morris porch," replied Mr. Simpkin coldly. "I was in and out of the Morris house all morning, supervising the removal of furniture. If it had been there, I would have seen it!"

"Well, I ain't no fool Mr. Simpkin, and I put that baby there with my own hands," said Margie, not certain she liked this man after all. At first, she had thought he was awfully handsome and sophisticated, but now she wasn't so sure. "I was only gone for a minute, to get his bottle, and when I came back he was gone! I thought you took him. Ma thought so too."

Her words were greeted by shocked silence. For her part, Rachel would have been ashamed to admit it, but she felt a sort of deliverance at the girl's disclosure. "The baby is missing?" she managed to squeak out, and Mrs. Potts patted her on the shoulder, mistaking her thinly veiled relief for concern.

Mr. Simpkin closed his eyes. He could feel a migraine coming on. Why did this have to happen to him?

"Both you and your mother are mistaken, my dear girl." His voice started to rise. "I certainly did not take the blasted baby anywhere!"

"Well, someone did," insisted Margie. "'Cause the basket's gone all right!"

"What basket?" he asked.

"The one the baby was in, of course," replied Margie.

"The only basket I saw on the porch was filled with old blankets," said Mr. Simpkin tersely.

"It weren't just blankets in that basket!" said a very excited Margie Purdy. "The baby was in there too!"

Mr. Simpkin turned on his heel and strode out of the store. Margie Purdy, Constable Jeffries and Rachel followed him. Mr. Lawson put down his broom and dustpan and sat across from his wife in front of the potbellied stove. He patted her knee and shook his head.

Outside, the group gathered around the cart. After inspecting its contents thoroughly, an exasperated Mr. Simpkin ran his fingers through his slicked-back hair and pointed to the rear of the cart. "There was a basket of blankets right there. I saw it." His hand traveled from his hair down the side of his face. This could not be happening.

Rachel stepped forward menacingly, her beribboned and feathered black hat looking quite incongruous above her egg-stained face. "Mr. Simpkin!" she announced. "If any harm has come to that baby I shall personally see that you never practice law on this Island again!"

Chapter Eleven

Sara sat in the hay, cradling the baby, singing softly to it. The sun's light had grown thin, and the air was much cooler than it had been when they had first arrived with the baby. She had soothed him to the point where he was nearly asleep, and gently she attempted to place him back in his basket. The minute she let go of him and tucked his covers around him, he started to cry fiercely. Sara quickly scooped him up, not daring to think what would happen if Uncle Alec were to come into the barn and find them. The baby gurgled and cooed as Sara cuddled him. She could have sworn that a little smile came to his lips as he looked up into her eyes, and she sat back down in the hay, absolutely entranced. A movement on the wooden stairs leading up to the loft startled her, but she let out a sigh of relief as Felicity's head appeared.

"It's just me," she said, seeing the fear on Sara's face.

The baby started to whimper softly again and Sara rocked him to and fro, amazed at her newly acquired abilities with babies. "Look!" she said to Felicity, proudly. "I almost got him to go to sleep! Isn't he beautiful?"

Felicity was more concerned with the problems at hand, and she started emptying her apron of all the booty she had managed to spirit away from her house.

"I got blankets and nappies and I brought

some milk. I found an old vinegar jar and a nipple that fits on top."

"Yecchh," said Sara.

"Don't worry. I washed it out. But it's the perfect size. Here, give him to me."

Sara reluctantly handed the baby to Felicity, who expertly held the vinegar bottle full of milk to his mouth. He started to suck hungrily. Sara watched in fascination, but Felicity began to look worried once again.

"Do you really think we did the right thing, Sara? Maybe we should take him back to that lawyer."

"Are you dreaming, Felicity King?" said Sara, her eyes as wide as saucers. "He'd just give it to Rachel Lynde. Can you imagine? The poor little thing. It would be a fate worse than death."

"Well," said Felicity, "I hope you've figured out a plan. We can't just go up to their door and say 'Hello, Malcolm. Here's a baby for you.'"

Sara realized there was some truth in what Felicity said. She would have to think of something, some way for this all to work out.

After a moment's pause, as the baby gurgled and grunted with pleasure, enjoying his milk, Sara's eyes lit up with a brilliant idea. "I know, Felicity! You could bring Abigail or Malcolm down to the pond and then I could float the baby over to you in its basket, just like Moses in the bulrushes!"

Felicity looked at her with alarm. "Don't be ridiculous Sara, he might drown!" The baby seemed to share her anxiety as he looked up at them both with serious blue eyes.

Sara nodded, her face falling. Felicity was right. It was too dangerous. But it was such a romantic idea.

"Besides," Felicity continued, "We have to do something tonight. And we have to do it really soon. It's too cold to keep him here." As if to prove her point, the wind howled a bit through the chinks of the barn walls, and they both shivered involuntarily.

Sara's hair glowed in the remaining sunshine of the day, and a twinkle came to her eyes as she looked at Felicity. "Well then, why don't we just leave him on their doorstep?"

Felicity bit her bottom lip. "Under the cover of darkness!" she added, their minds in harmony.

"With a note!" finished Sara triumphantly, barely able to contain her joy. They grinned conspiratorially and shook hands on it.

Chapter Twelve

The lamps were lit and the fire was glowing as Abigail sewed in her little parlor, ensconced in her favorite chair. It was good to be home. She sighed and looked around the room appreciatively. She had finally conquered the chaos and things were where back where they should be. The fire in the grate made shadows dance on the walls, and the wind rattled the windows. Still, she was not completely content. If only she and Malcolm had not had those words.

As if reading her mind, Malcolm entered from the kitchen. He looked quite downcast as he quietly surveyed the room. "I think I might take a little air," he announced after a moment's silence. He waited for Abigail's response, but there was none. "Care to come for a stroll with me?" he asked, stalling in the doorway.

"No thank you," replied Abigail primly, concentrating on her stitching.

Malcolm watched her, her auburn head bent over her sewing in the golden light of the fire, and he longed to just go over and scoop her up and cover her with kisses. Instead, he took a deep breath, shrugged and left the parlor.

By the front door, Malcolm took down his heavy cardigan from its hook. He paused and looked back into the parlor. Abigail continued to sew.

Outside, the wind whistled through the pines that formed a windbreak between the surrounding fields and Abigail and Malcolm's house. The lights of the house spilled out onto the lawn and were a welcome sight to Sara and Felicity as they finally made their way out of the darkness of the bush, carrying the heavy basket between them. They could see the lamps on in the parlor and the buggy in the driveway. They nodded at each other and smiled. The stage was set.

They crept forward, holding onto the basket very carefully. They slipped up the walk between the little rosebushes. Suddenly, Malcolm's shadow crossed in front of the window. Their hearts skipped a beat and they ducked behind a bush in front of the white picket fence to avoid being seen. Just in the nick of time too, for the door opened, and Malcolm appeared. Just as he was about to step outside onto the walk, the sound of Abigail's voice came from the house.

"Malcolm!" she called.

Malcolm stopped and went back inside, shutting the door after him.

Felicity and Sara breathed a sigh of relief, but their moment of relaxation was short-lived. The baby awoke and started to cry. Frantically, they rocked the basket back and forth, not daring to look into each other's eyes for fear of giving up on their plan entirely.

Malcolm entered the parlor. Abigail put away her sewing and stood stiffly looking at him, her blue eyes betraying her real feelings. "Maybe I will come with you..." she said haltingly.

Malcolm beamed. "Good. Make sure you wear something warm. There's a real chill in the air tonight."

"My wrap is in the kitchen." Abigail smiled at him and went to fetch it.

The minute the baby was relatively calm, Felicity and Sara tiptoed back along the path to the doorway and placed the basket on the steps. The baby started crying the minute they let go of the handles. Sara bent down to comfort him, but Felicity grabbed her hand and pulled her off into the darkness.

Malcolm was standing in the little hallway, waiting for Abigail, when he heard a slight noise outside the door. For a brief second he thought it must be the wind, but after years of sleeping outside in the bush in his mining days, he was acutely aware of any little sound, especially ones that were out of place with his surroundings. The sound repeated itself, and this time he moved towards the door with a furrowed brow and peered out the window.

"What in...?" he exclaimed and opened the door.

He stared down at the basket in wonder. Then he strode out into the yard. "Hey now!" he called. "Anybody out there? Come forward!"

He stood there in the silence, seeing and hearing no one. Shaking his head, he slowly walked back to the basket. Surely his eyes had been playing tricks on him. He stood, towering above it, and looked down in amazement, hardly daring to accept what his eyes could plainly see. As beautiful a baby as you would ever hope to behold, red-cheeked and blue-eyed.

The baby was crying with great gusto by now and Malcolm felt a pounding in his chest, quite unlike anything he had ever experienced before. He heard the door open behind him and Abigail's sharp intake of breath as she took in the scene.

❧

Malcolm stopped reading.
"Now what do you make of that?" he asked in a voice
that was much more controlled than his face.
It was obvious that he was quite moved,
and determined not to show it.

꘏꘏꘏

"I'm here because I have a bone to pick with you,
Rachel Lynde!" Hetty stated coldly and clearly.
"I've heard all the stories in town!
But then you never fooled me!
You didn't really want this baby at all, did you?"

❧❧❧

"And do you remember how all
the other boys called him 'owl-eyes'?"
Rachel let out a snort.
"It was because of those glasses he wore!"
She and Hetty started to laugh so hard,
tears came to their eyes.

❧

"Now calm yourself, Rachel," said Hetty,
taking charge of the situation.
"The child is all frazzled because the two of us
are in such a tizzy.
I know from my teaching experience never to let a
child know what you're really feeling."

"Malcolm! What...? It's a baby!" she stuttered, in disbelief.

"Yes. It's a baby," said Malcolm matter-of-factly as he picked up the basket and carried it into the house. Abigail, her eyes wide with confusion, looked around the yard once again, and then followed Malcolm inside.

Unseen, in the bushes, Sara and Felicity hugged each other in barely controlled glee, certain in their innocent belief that their plan had worked and all was well.

Chapter Thirteen

Abigail paced frantically about the parlor, still trying to come to grips with the situation.

"But where...? Oh Malcolm—" She stopped suddenly, and looked at him with eyes that betrayed the thought that had passed unbidden through her mind. "You haven't anything to do with this, have you?" she asked haltingly, hoping that her suspicions would not be confirmed.

"Abby, I swear, I have no idea where it has come from!" said Malcolm, gently placing the basket down on the settee.

Abigail closed her eyes in relief, but they flew

open as the reality of the situation hit her once again. "What are we going to do?" she cried in complete panic. She jumped in alarm as the baby howled loudly.

"Well, I suppose we should take it out of the basket to start! It doesn't seem to be too happy," replied Malcolm calmly as he parted the blankets covering the crying infant. Gently, he lifted the baby out and the crying stopped. As he did so, his eyes were drawn to a sheet of notepaper that poked out between the blankets and the side of the basket. Balancing the child on his hip, he leaned down and plucked it out.

"What's this? Here, hold the baby Abigail," he said, handing the baby to his wife.

Abigail backed away, cringing at the thought of holding it. "Oh, I couldn't, Malcolm. Babies don't like me!" She looked at the little creature in astonishment and instantly he began to howl again. She looked up at Malcolm pleadingly.

"Hold the baby, Abby," he said, and firmly pressed him into Abigail's arms. She took him reluctantly, holding him out from her body as if he were made of china and she were afraid that any movement would break it. Amazingly, he stopped crying and matched Abigail's puzzled look with his own.

Malcolm slowly unfolded the piece of paper. It was a note, obviously scribbled so that the handwriting would not be identifiable. He began to read: "I am an orphaned baby boy. I am bound for a fate worse than death in an orphanage, or even worse, a home without love. I know you can take good care of me. Please keep me."

Malcolm stopped reading. "Now, what do you make of that?" he asked in a voice that was much more controlled than his face. It was obvious that he was quite moved, and determined not to show it.

Abigail knew that look. It was the same one he had worn when he'd brought the cradle into the house to show her.

"Now don't get all sentimental about this, Malcolm. He has to belong to someone. He did not just drop out of the night sky! We have to report it!"

"Well," said Malcolm slowly, not quite wanting to meet her eyes, "it's too late to take him anywhere tonight."

The baby cried suddenly again, and twisted and turned in Abigail's arms. "Would you please hold it, Malcolm. I'm afraid I'm going to drop it," Abigail begged, holding the baby out.

"Hand the wee thing to me," said Malcolm calmly. The baby quietened as Malcolm joggled it up and down. "He's a handsome little fellow. You'll grant him that, won't you Abby?"

Malcolm looked down at the baby in his arms with undisguised wonder as Abigail looked at the pair of them in horror.

Chapter Fourteen

Clouds scudded across the night sky and hid the moon from sight as Felicity and Sara said a whispered goodnight at the King farm. The house was in darkness. A chilling wind rustled through the falling leaves and flung them against the veranda, where they stuck in the trellises, the bare, winding tendrils of clematis still stubbornly clinging there.

"Sara, I'm scared," Felicity confessed with a shiver as she was just about to sneak in through the kitchen door.

"What is there to be afraid of?" asked Sara, with more bravado than she felt, pulling her coat around her more tightly.

"What if we get arrested for kidnapping the baby?"

Sara took a deep breath. Trust Felicity to come right to the point.

"We won't. When they find out the baby is perfectly happy with Malcolm and Abigail, everything will be forgiven."

"I hope so," replied Felicity with a sigh.

"I'd better go," said Sara, not particularly wanting to pursue the conversation. Felicity had echoed the very thing that she had been brooding about ever since they had run a safe distance from Abigail's. The excitement and exhilaration of the moment had worn off and had been replaced by a nagging unrest.

Sara waved and hurried away as Felicity let herself quietly into the house. The wind blew the leaves around her ankles as she ran down the driveway towards Rose Cottage. She hoped fervently that both her Aunt Hetty and Aunt Olivia were long since asleep.

Of course they had done the right thing, she scolded herself. She and Felicity had saved that baby from untold misery. She smiled, her face to the wind, and remembered the look on Malcolm's face when he first looked down on the baby in the basket. Even from their hideout in the bushes, it had been clear as day what his feelings were. She imagined the scene back at Abigail and Malcolm's house and gave a little hop and a skip along the road. They're probably happier tonight than they have been in their whole lives, she thought to herself with satisfaction.

Chapter Fifteen

If Sara had been a fly on the wall at Abigail's house, she would have seen that her rosy daydream was not exactly the way things were in reality.

The baby wriggled and cried in Abigail's arms as she frantically paced back and forth across her little parlor. She was at her wits' end. The baby had not ceased wailing for what seemed to be the past hour. She looked this way and that around the room, as if the answer to the infant's woes might be written somewhere, plain to see. Her arms felt as if they were going to fall off. The child was not undernourished, that was for sure. He was a healthy weight.

She set him down on the settee and stretched her arms. She looked around, deciding which of her cushions she could risk using as a barrier. She spotted an old one that Great-aunt Priscilla had made for her. She had always meant to recover it with a more tasteful fabric. As she crossed the room to fetch it, she glimpsed the baby beginning to roll off the couch. Abigail gasped and raced back to the settee, tripping over a small table she had forgotten she'd moved. She reached the baby in the nick of time, catching him as he threatened to hurtle into space. She gingerly lifted him up and, awkwardly cradling him in her arms, sat down herself, her heart beating wildly. She rose up quickly enough though, realizing that the settee was soaked, and so, indeed, was her skirt.

Abigail let out a small cry of despair and carried the infant into the kitchen. She looked around in dismay and her shoulders drooped. The kitchen was an absolute mess. The baby's blankets hung on a line to warm in front of the wood stove, and the dinner dishes were still drying on the sideboard. Malcolm had promised to put them away while she sewed, but obviously he had set out for his stroll before he'd got around to them.

She headed to the sink for a cloth to sponge the settee, but the only one available was sitting in the dishwater where Malcolm had left it, soaking wet. She always wrung the dishcloth out and hung it neatly over the pump to dry when she finished with it, but as many times as she had told him, Malcolm never seemed to remember to do this.

She stood for a moment with the dripping cloth in her hand, wondering how in heaven's name she could wring it out while still holding onto a squirming, crying baby. Finally, she put him over her shoulder and attempted to balance him there while she got a strong hold on the cloth.

The baby let out an extra loud scream of protest and Abigail threw the rag back into the dirty water in the sink and called out with exasperation, "Malcolm MacEwan! Where are you? You promised you'd help me!"

Malcolm entered the kitchen from outside, carrying the white wicker cradle. "Abby, what is it?" he asked cheerfully. Abigail stared at the cradle and then at Malcolm. The baby squirmed in her stiff arms, screaming and crying. "Fate must have led me to that auction, don't you think?" he said, a wry smile on his handsome face.

"You'd try the patience of a saint, Malcolm MacEwan. If I didn't know you to be an honest man, I'd still think you had a hand in this." She managed a faint smile and Malcolm smiled back. The baby howled and the mood was gone.

"I have never felt so helpless in all my life," wailed Abigail. "Do you think he's just hungry?"

"He can't be," replied Malcolm. "He won't eat! I tried him on the porridge."

"Porridge! Well, no wonder the little thing is crying!" Abigail was aghast. You didn't feed a babe this age oatmeal! Even she knew that much.

Malcolm reached for the baby. "Here, let me have him. You're probably holding him too tight."

Abigail turned away from Malcolm's outstretched arms. "I'm not holding him too tight! He's just fine," she retorted, but the baby cried even harder and, changing her mind, she handed him over gladly. "Do you think he's sick?" Abigail fretted as she felt the baby's face and hands. "See how hot his little hands and feet are?"

"Well of course he's hot. He's been lying by the fire, lass."

"No, no, Malcolm," Abigail insisted. "Look! He's flushed!"

"Don't fuss so, Abby. He's flushed because he's been crying!" All of a sudden, the cause of the baby's distress soaked through the heavy layers of Malcolm's shirt. "And he's crying because he's soaking wet! Bring me one of those nappies."

Abigail stood stock-still. "Malcolm! I've never changed a baby in my life!"

Chapter Sixteen

The wind continued to howl and buffet the tall pines around the dark and silent house. The last buds of the miniature rosebushes scudded along the path and were lost among the maple and oak leaves.

The grandfather clock in the darkened parlor struck three, its toll faintly reaching the second-story bedroom where Malcolm slept soundly and Abigail's eyes finally closed to rest. The little white wicker cradle sat in the corner of the room, looking almost as if it had always been there. It began to rock gently in the moonlight and a sudden cry pierced the silence.

Abigail sat up abruptly, almost as if she were a puppet whose strings had been pulled by an invisible master. Her heart leapt into her throat and she jumped out of bed and stumbled over to the cradle, the floor like ice beneath her bare feet. She picked up the baby with ease, too exhausted to worry whether she was doing it properly or not.

"Oh, you're not crying again!" she whispered, cuddling him. "I just got to sleep."

She groped around in the darkness for his bottle. Finding it, she sat down on the chair next to the cradle and shifted the baby into her lap. The baby stopped crying and looked at her, and she could have sworn that a tiny smile lit up his face in the darkness.

Abigail stared back, transfixed, and found herself smiling back tentatively. "Shh. There, there," she cooed, unexpectedly confident as she put the bottle in the baby's mouth. "Were you lonely? Don't worry. We're here. Nobody is going to let you be lonely."

The infant sucked greedily as she looked down at him, and his great blue eyes fixed on her.

Malcolm, awakened too, watched the pair silently in awe, admiring his wife's beautiful hair lying loose about her shoulders as she bent over the baby, cooing and scolding softly.

The baby dropped off to sleep and Abigail put him very gently back into his cradle. She tiptoed towards her bed, looking very proud of herself. She realized suddenly that Malcolm was awake and watching her, and she slid into bed into the comfort of his arms. But no sooner had she lain her head on the pillow than the baby started to howl again.

Abigail sat up in bed in frustration, but Malcolm patted her shoulder. "Here, Abby," he said, getting out of bed. "Let me take him."

"What am I supposed to do?" Abigail was almost in tears as she followed Malcolm over to the cradle. "I haven't had a wink of sleep. I don't know what to do! He was fine a second ago. How does he know the minute I leave him?"

Malcolm reached into the cradle and drew the sobbing baby out. "Well, it's just like a pup I had up north," said Malcolm softly, patting the baby on the back in a rhythmic fashion. "Took it away from its mother too soon and it whined all night long for the first three weeks. All right now, you go back to bed. I'll hold him."

Abigail went back to bed thankfully and pulled the blankets up to her nose, shivering. She watched as Malcolm rocked and dipped the baby in an odd circling fashion. "Whatever are you doing, Malcolm MacEwan?" she asked.

"Panning for gold," replied Malcolm. "He seems to like it."

The effect in fact was nothing short of miraculous. The baby stopped crying and settled down to sleep. Malcolm sat down quietly in the chair and stared at the sleeping infant.

The sun rose from the sea, sending pink and mauve streaks across its surface. The waves lapped gently on the shore. The wind of the night had died, but it had brought a new chill to the air, and its cold crispness had about it a definite scent of the coming winter.

The sun shone through the lace curtains of Abigail's front window. As she came down the stairs, yawning and hollow-eyed, still in her long, white flannel nightgown.

"Malcolm," she called quietly, wondering where he had disappeared to so early in the morning. The baby was not in its cradle either.

She opened the parlor door quietly and peeked in. There was Malcolm, sound asleep in the rocking chair. His arms were folded around the baby who lay contentedly on his chest under his nightshirt. Abigail stood quite still in the doorway, and tears slowly welled up in her eyes.

Chapter Seventeen

It was one of those perfect autumn days, not a cloud in the azure-blue sky. The sun was throwing just enough warmth that, while coats were put on for the benefit of parents' who warned about sore throats and the influenza season, they were hastily thrown off at the first chance. The wind had died down, and the air was so crisp and new you felt that you were breathing for the first time.

Felicity and Sara sped across the field, only their heads visible above the tips of the long golden grass. They passed through the wind-break of tall green pines and came upon the clearing where Abigail's house stood. The second thoughts and fears of the night before were for the most part forgotten as they skipped along the neat little path to the house. As they arrived at the door, the sound of a baby crying reached their ears.

"Isn't that a lovely sound?" said Sara, stuffing her tam in her pocket, grinning with pleasure. Felicity was still not quite so sure.

"Now remember," whispered Sara excitedly, "we don't know anything." Felicity nodded, her usual self-confidence shaken. Sara knocked on the door. She turned to Felicity, biting her bottom lip, her eyes sparkling with anticipation.

After what seemed like forever to the two girls, a shadow appeared behind the lace curtain, the handle turned and the door opened.

Abigail stood in the doorway, not looking at all like the Abigail they remembered. Her usually impeccable hair was held up with only a few pins, allowing strands and wisps to escape from their hold. The front of her white blouse had a small stain on it of indeterminate nature, and most of all, the bright blue eyes, always so intelligent and full of life, were dull with the need for sleep and rimmed with pale purple. The girls found themselves staring rudely at her.

"Oh," she said, as if she were trying to find their names in the recesses of her mind. "Felicity, Sara. How nice to see you." Except it sounded strangely as if it were not that nice to see them—in fact, quite the opposite. She smiled bravely. "Come in."

Sara and Felicity looked at each other and followed her through the door, even forgetting to wipe their feet. And, what was more unbelievable, Abigail forgot to ask them to.

The two girls looked around the little front hall expectantly and strained to see through into the parlor. They waited to see if Abigail would invite them to take their coats off, but she just stood to one side, watching them as if in a daze. Sara took the initiative and pulled her coat off, hanging it neatly on the peg beside the door. Felicity did the same.

"We just couldn't wait to visit and find out how your trip was," said Sara brightly as Felicity nodded, not daring to say anything.

"Trip?" said Abigail, coming back to reality. "The trip? Oh...it was fine, dear. Yes, the trip was fine. Thank you!" She looked distractedly towards the kitchen door at the end of the hall, almost as if she had a premonition of what would happen next. From behind the closed door of the kitchen came a singular wail.

Sara looked at Abigail, her blue eyes wide with innocence. "What was that?"

"A baby, Sara," replied Abigail flatly.

"A baby?" Sara echoed in feigned amazement, and looked knowingly at Felicity.

Chapter Eighteen

The kitchen was unrecognizable. Rows of clean nappies dried over the wood stove on makeshift clotheslines that were strung from hooks in the ceiling, hooks that had previously provided neat storage for bunches of herbs and sparkling pots and pans. Baby bottles soaked in a large kettle on top of the stove, and the sideboard was covered in cloths and blankets, creating a temporary change table.

Sara and Felicity sat around the kitchen table with shocked looks on their faces. Things were certainly not as they had expected they would be.

The only one who appeared to be rested and contented was the baby, who looked around happily at all his guests from the comfort of the crook of Malcolm's arm.

"All I know is that we have to find out who left him here," Abigail was saying. "It's absolutely dreadful not knowing. And I don't think I'm able to give him the care he needs. Someone like your mother, Felicity, would be much better able to." Aunt Abigail's words flowed out, one on top of the other, her insecurity building to a fever pitch.

Malcolm patted her arm with his one free hand. "Oh now, Abby, you're doing just fine," he said soothingly.

"Well, they always say the first night with any new baby is always the worst," said Sara brightly.

Abigail went on as if she hadn't heard her. "It's horrible! There wasn't a moment I wasn't in fear for his very life." She leaned her elbow on the table—something that Abigail would never, never do—and put her head on her hand. "I keep telling you, Malcolm, we have to report this to Abner Jeffries. He might know something that we don't."

"It'll be a cold day on the equator when Abner Jeffries knows something that I don't," Malcolm declared explosively. The baby's eyes flew open, but instead of crying at Malcolm's outburst, a tiny toothless smile lit up his face.

"Oh, look at his little smile," cooed Sara.

"What are we going to do?" demanded Abigail.

Sara turned from playing peek-a-boo with the baby. "Maybe if you gave it just one more night," she began, tentatively.

Again, it was almost as if she hadn't spoken.

"Malcolm, please! We've got to do something!" Abigail wailed.

Malcolm looked at his wife's tired, anxious, almost ashen face and realized there was nothing else to be done. He rose slowly. "All right, I'll go. I realize we have to try to find out where he came from," he said, with far more conviction than he felt. Sara and Felicity looked at each other dejectedly.

"Come on, lassies. I'll drop you off home on my way." The two girls very grudgingly stood up to leave.

Malcolm handed the baby to Abigail. She shrank away from him slightly, but he cooed and gurgled and wriggled his way into a more comfortable position.

"There you go, Lucky!" said Malcolm, seeing

that both Abigail and the baby were relatively comfortable.

"What did you call him?" asked Abigail.

"Oh...uh, Lucky," said Malcolm, putting his arm into his coat sleeve. "You remember that pup I told you about at the mine? We called it Lucky." Malcolm continued to put on his coat.

Abigail was flabbergasted. "Don't you dare call this baby by a dog's name!"

Malcolm stopped mid-sleeve and looked at her with surprise. A slight twinkle came to his eye, but he replaced it with a serious expression. "Come along, my girls!" he said as he herded Felicity and Sara out the door, but not before they gave one last sad look at the baby in Abigail's arms.

The house was very silent after their footsteps had faded away. Abigail looked down at the little figure in her arms. He had dozed off, his long golden lashes resting on his chubby pink cheeks.

"That's a boy," said Abigail softly, pulling his blanket around him more securely. "You had quite a night too, didn't you? Yes you did." Then, her head jerked up, and she wondered where in heaven those words had ever come from.

Chapter Nineteen

Night rested peacefully on the village of Avonlea. The stars twinkled, an owl hooted, and the chickens in the henhouse at Rose Cottage tucked their heads under their wings. The porch swing rocked gently back and forth in the light breeze, and leaves that had escaped the vigorous sweeping that Hetty King had given the porch that afternoon blew into the corners, making a delicate scratching sound.

The lamps were still lit in the kitchen of Rose Cottage, shining warmly and comfortingly in the darkness, but all was not peace and light inside.

Upstairs, in the little room that looked over the porch roof, Sara Stanley lay in bed, comforter up to her chin, her eyes wide open, staring at the shadows the tree branches threw on the flowered wallpaper of her ceiling. Usually she enjoyed watching the different shapes dancing and twirling, almost like the dervishes she had seen on one of her trips to India with her father, so long ago. But tonight was different. Tonight she was filled with a sadness she hadn't felt for months. She wondered what her father might be doing, whether it was nighttime in Montreal, if he were asleep or awake. Maybe he was sitting in his office, poring over papers at his big desk, the green lamp spreading a pool of light over his work and his handsome features. Tears sprang into her eyes. She missed him so much.

But she discovered suddenly that she wasn't just crying for her own loneliness, she was crying for the baby's as well. What would happen to him now? Maybe she had been wrong. Maybe she shouldn't have interfered. She should have simply let fate take its course. Perhaps things were, as Mrs. Lynde had said so many times, preordained. She sat up and punched her pillow several times. No matter what she did to it tonight, it refused to be comfortable.

Downstairs in the kitchen, her Aunt Olivia took the kettle off the stove and poured the boiling water into a china teapot. Hetty entered quietly from the parlor and sat down at the table, wearily rubbing her eyes. She had been correcting mathematics exercises, but her heart was not in it. Perhaps a cup of tea will revive me, she thought.

Her younger sister looked at her, her brown eyes filled with concern.

"Hetty, you didn't touch your food at dinner. Please, have a cup of tea and a biscuit with me."

"I have no appetite, Olivia," replied Hetty wearily. "But, yes. I will have a cup of tea."

The two sisters were as different as night and day. Olivia was the younger of the two by twenty years. Her face was fresh and innocent, full of the idealistic dreams of someone quite untouched by life. Hetty always accused her of living on dreams, not reality, and perhaps there was some truth in this. However, Olivia's kindly, warm, almost childlike disposition left little room for criticism.

"You're not still fretting about Rachel Lynde, are you?" she asked as she set a cup and saucer down in front of Hetty.

"I'm far more worried about poor Jane's baby than I am about Rachel Lynde," Hetty snapped. "They haven't found it yet, you know."

"Oh, I know. The town is full of talk. It's absolutely dreadful," said Olivia. "When I think it might be out in the dark somewhere...in the woods, cold and helpless and hungry...or worse..." Olivia's eyes filled with misery at the thoughts stirring in her vivid imagination.

"Olivia! Please!" said Hetty, with some annoyance.

Sara could hear their voices quite clearly through the grate in her floor that allowed the heat to rise into her room from the kitchen. She got out of bed and, shivering, knelt on the cold floor and peered through its opening.

"You don't suppose someone could have taken him, do you?" her Aunt Olivia was saying.

Aunt Hetty got up from the table and proceeded to pace back and forth across the room, much as she did in front of the blackboard at school, Sara thought.

"Heaven knows what kind of person would take a baby and not tell anyone about it!" she declared. "But if that is the case, the scoundrel ought to be thrown into jail for the rest of his natural born days!"

Sara sat back abruptly, her heart beating wildly, her face white in the moonlight.

Olivia took a tray of fresh, hot tea biscuits from the stove and set them to cool on the sideboard. She looked at Hetty where she stood, ramrod straight, with her back to her. Hetty never invited comfort, but Olivia could see it was one of those times when she needed it. She went over to her sister and touched her gently on the arm. "I'm sure there's a mistake. No one could be that thoughtless and cruel. Come and have a tea biscuit. They're fresh out of the oven."

Hetty allowed herself to be led to the table

and she sank down into her chair with her head in her hands. Olivia patted her sister's shoulder. "Here, have some tea."

Upstairs, Sara's heart filled with remorse. She stood up, knowing there was something she had to do. She hesitated only a moment and then went to the door, opened it and walked into the darkness of the hallway. She tiptoed down the stairs and headed to where a sliver of light shone around the kitchen door. She stopped and looked through the crack.

Her Aunt Hetty was still sitting at the table, rubbing her temples, deep in thought. Olivia sipped her tea, sitting with her back to the door.

Sara took a deep breath and entered. "Aunt Hetty," she said quietly.

Hetty jumped in her chair, startled out of her reverie. "Oh good heavens, child, you gave me quite a fright! What are you doing, wandering around in the middle of the night?"

Olivia leapt up to cover Sara's shoulders with a plaid shawl that hung over the back of a chair.

"Sara, you'll catch your death!"

"I couldn't sleep," mumbled Sara. "I was thinking about that poor little baby."

"So were we," said Hetty quietly, sipping her tea.

Sara swallowed hard, trying desperately to

think how she could put what she wanted to say into words.

"Aunt Hetty, what if someone had taken the baby because they knew of someone...who didn't really know it themselves...but they would make wonderful parents. Wouldn't that be a good reason to do something that seems so wrong to everyone else?"

Hetty's head slowly rose from her cup of tea. "What are you trying to say, child," she asked slowly, staring at Sara intently.

"Well," Sara took a deep breath, "if the person who took the baby gave it to these people who loved it and everything turned out fine in the end...would that person still be in real trouble?"

Hetty tugged on her earlobe with some anxiety. "I don't happen to know this person, do I, Sara?"

"Yes..." replied Sara meekly.

Hetty clasped her hands together on the table top, almost as if she were saying grace. "Sara Stanley!" she finally said. "Tell me you don't have anything to do with all this...do you...?"

Sara bit her bottom lip. Then, in a rush, she blurted out the whole story to an increasingly astonished and shocked Hetty and Olivia.

"We thought the baby should have a mother and a father who really wanted it, who really loved it. Babies know these things. They know when they're really wanted and when they're not. We didn't want Rachel Lynde to have the baby!" Sara, having said everything there was to say, waited for her aunt's reaction.

Olivia stood quite still by the stove, her mouth open. "Oh Sara! What have you done?" she squeaked.

Hetty's face had completely drained of any color it had once had, but she remained seated at the table, her hands still firmly clasped.

"Who," she demanded quietly, "is 'we'?"

"Felicity and I," replied a chastened Sara.

Hetty shot out of her chair and started to pace. "Oh my good lord, I should have known! You didn't want Rachel Lynde to have the baby," she repeated Sara's words, and there seemed almost to be a note of triumph amidst the anxiety.

"We...uh, really didn't think you should have it either, Aunt Hetty," said Sara, with some hesitation. If she was setting things to rights, she wanted the whole thing on the table.

Hetty stopped in her tracks and looked at Sara indignantly. "I beg your pardon?"

"Oh, Aunt Hetty, I'm sorry if you're angry with me, but...you just wanted the baby because you didn't want Rachel Lynde to have it." Hetty's mouth dropped but Sara went on before she could interrupt her. "Now, Malcolm and Abigail needed a baby. That's why we gave it to them."

"You gave the Morris baby to Malcolm and Abigail?" uttered a stunned Hetty.

"Well, they don't exactly know who gave it to them..." stammered Sara.

Hetty sat back down at the table quite abruptly and rubbed her temples with her fingers.

"But Sara!" said Olivia, still unable to believe all that she had heard with her own ears. "Someone has to be told!"

Sara's lower lip started to tremble. "Malcolm already did! He told Abner Jeffries this afternoon, so everything is all spoiled!" She paused, trying very hard not to cry. "I'm sorry I didn't tell you sooner. I hated to see you so upset. But...I'm...I'm not sorry I did it," she finished defiantly.

A mixture of emotions crossed over Hetty's face. As Sara stood before her, her thin shoulders back and her chin jutted out, she was the very image of her mother, Ruth.

Ruth had been much more than Hetty's favorite little sister. She had been almost like her own child. Their mother had not been very well after Ruth was born, and Hetty had brought her up. A child so strong-willed and certain of her own destiny that Hetty had finally, unwillingly, had to let her go. Only to lose her. Her own eyes filled with tears, remembering, but she was not one to show any emotions whatsoever, if she could help it, and she returned her thoughts to the matter at hand. What anger she felt because Sara had done such a thing and had not told her sooner was tempered greatly by her relief that the baby was safe and sound.

"Sara Stanley, you will be the death of me," she finally said as she rose from the table. "In the morning, I want the whole story from the beginning. Now go back to bed this instant!"

Sara breathed a sigh of relief. "Goodnight Aunt Hetty. Goodnight Aunt Olivia. I feel much better. Now that I've bared my soul, I think I can sleep," she said as she left the room.

Hetty watched her go, shaking her head. "The sleep of the just," she commented drily.

"At least the child is safe, Hetty," said Olivia, cautiously amazed at her sister's outwardly calm demeanor.

"Not if Rachel Lynde gets him," said Hetty decisively, and Olivia realized that the war was only just starting.

Chapter Twenty

"Look! Malcolm! He's finished all this milk! He had a much better night last night. Didn't you? Yes you did."

The baby's face was wreathed in dimples as he stared up at Abigail from his comfortable spot in the crook of her arm.

"Oh look, he smiled at me! Did you see that, Malcolm? He really did!" Abigail watched in fascination to see if it really were a smile or only a bit of gas from drinking his milk so quickly.

Malcolm smiled and looked over at her, sitting in the rocking chair they had brought from the parlor to the kitchen. They had both agreed that the view out the kitchen window was far prettier, and the baby seemed to enjoy watching the wind blow through the tall pines that stood in a row next to the golden field.

But Malcolm's smile did not last. Ever since his meeting of the day before with Abner Jeffries, he had been brooding, his mind preoccupied. He had tried to look upon the whole situation realistically, knowing that he had done the right thing, telling himself that this was best for him and for Abigail, and their marriage. But they both knew that Mr. Simpkin would very soon be knocking on their door, and the closer the time came, the more difficult it was to look at things realistically.

"What a big boy to drink all that milk," cooed Abigail, patting the baby's back as he lay comfortably over her shoulder. "Yes you are."

There was a great pounding on the front door. Both Abigail and Malcolm froze and looked at each other. Malcolm finally rose to his feet and went to answer the knock. Abigail carried the baby to the sink and, still patting his back, looked out the window quietly, trying to understand and control her emotions. The sound of voices came from the front hall.

Malcolm towered over Mr. Simpkin as the young lawyer explained more of the facts of the case to him, facts that Malcolm really did not want to hear but Mr. Simpkin felt it his duty to relay to him. Abner Jeffries stood in the background, his chest puffed out with the sheer power vested in him by the community of Avonlea.

"Rachel Lynde is, in fact, the infant's next of kin, and she has led me to believe that she will provide a home for him," Mr. Simpkin said, finding himself strangely intimidated by this tall man who stood before him. Who did he think he was?

He was acting as if they were stealing the baby from him, when it was very obviously the other way around.

An ashen-faced Abigail entered the front hall with the child in her arm, and stood behind Malcolm. "Rachel Lynde?" she said, disbelief and disappointment apparent in her voice. Not that she wasn't a fine, upstanding woman. But mothering an infant? Instinctively, Abigail held the baby tighter to her.

Abner stepped forward, feeling it was about time he had his say. "Abigail, I know how you must feel, but by law it's rightfully hers." He stepped back, very proud of the words of comfort he had chosen. He had been practicing them all the way over in the buggy.

Abigail looked at Malcolm and he nodded sadly. She passed the baby over to Abner in a kind of daze.

"Hello youngster," said Abner as he held the baby awkwardly. The baby answered him with a howl that set the man's hair on end. "Oh my, you're a noisy wee thing," he muttered, shifting the baby to a new position in hopes that it would stop the infernal crying.

"Here's his basket," Abigail said quietly, reaching down to where it lay in the hall. The basket he had arrived in. Was it really only two nights ago?

Constable Jeffries put the baby in the basket with much relief, but he continued to cry.

"Good day," said Mr. Simpkin crisply, almost clicking his heels. "Sorry for the inconvenience."

"Thank you for alerting us," said Abner, picking up the basket. "It took Simpkin here quite a while to sort out the question of custody."

Mr. Simpkin glared at the man, resenting his insinuation that he had somehow not measured up. Then the two men fumbled their way out the door, both trying to exit at the same time with the basket between them.

Abigail broke through from behind Malcolm and followed them out. "Tell Mrs. Lynde that he likes his milk just lukewarm, not cold and not hot!" she called out to them from the front steps as they lifted the basket up onto the buggy. Malcolm came and stood behind her, his hand on her shoulder.

Abner Jeffries nodded, even though he wasn't sure he'd caught her words over the howling.

Little did any of them realize that they were being watched. Hetty King had been walking up the path determinedly to pay a visit to Malcolm and Abigail. She had seen the buggy but assumed it was theirs. However, when she had seen the unmistakable shadows of Mr. Theodore Simpkin and Abner Jeffries through the lace curtains of the window, she had run and hidden in the very same bushes Sara and Felicity had used for cover two nights before. Unseen by all, she watched as Mr. Simpkin settled himself in the driver's seat, Abner beside him, a basket between them. The lawyer gave the reins a flick and the horse started to move forward.

Malcolm called after them, "Tell Mrs. Lynde the best way to get him to sleep is to hold him as if you were panning for gold!" Malcolm demonstrated the circular motion with his hands clasped together.

"I have never panned for gold, Mr. MacEwan," called back Mr. Simpkin disdainfully. "So I have no idea what you are talking about."

The buggy pulled away. Abigail broke into tears and Malcolm put his arm around her as they went back into the house. Hetty realized instantly what had happened.

"So, Rachel Lynde is to have the baby after all, is she?" she said to herself. "We'll see about that!" Hetty set off down the road on foot, in the direction the buggy had taken, as fast as her legs would carry her.

Chapter Twenty-One

Business was pretty much as usual in the Avonlea general store. A group of people were gathered around the old potbellied stove, warming their hands, gossiping and telling tales. Most of the stories, of course, concerned the disappearance of the Morris baby, which was still an unexplained mystery, thanks—to give credit where credit was due—to the discretion of Abner Jeffries and Mr. Simpkin. After Malcolm had visited them with his astonishing news, they had deemed it necessary to keep the discovery of the baby's whereabouts a secret until they actually had their hands on him. Then and only then, they had decided, would they notify his next of kin. Thus they hoped to avoid another confrontation of the type they had witnessed in the general store.

"Well, if it weren't so terrible it would be funny," whispered Mrs. Lawson to Mrs. Potts. "Theodore Simpkin moving the Morris baby along with the furniture, by mistake!"

"Doesn't surprise me," replied Mrs. Potts. "Theodore Simpkin wouldn't know a baby from a washboard!" The group surrounding her joined in with her whoops of laughter.

Meanwhile, Mr. Lawson was serving Mr. and Mrs. Biggins from the boarding house next door. Mr. Biggins leaned forward over the counter and said confidentially, "I hear Abner was out at the Sloane Farm lookin' down the well."

"Oh dear lord," breathed a horrified Mrs. Biggins. "He didn't find anything, did he?"

"Only old man Sloane's empty whiskey bottles!" said her husband, exploding into laughter along with Mr. Lawson, as his wife tittered behind her hand appreciatively.

Amidst all this frivolity, a very sombre Rachel Lynde entered the store, dressed from head to toe in black. The groups split apart as she swept her way to the counter towards a very uncomfortable looking Mr. Lawson. He and Rachel had not spoken two words since the episode of the egg and potato throwing.

Rachel was not one to beat about the bush. If she had something to say she always came straight to the point without meandering about it. She prided herself upon this trait. And come to the point she did, as she faced Mr. E. C. Lawson eye to eye across his counter.

"Rachel," greeted Mr. Lawson tentatively, and his wife quietly joined him.

"Edward," she returned. She cleared her

throat. "I'm not one that can't apologize when I know a wrong has been committed. Even though I was not the instigator, I would like to pay for any damage or loss that resulted the other day, and I apologize for my behavior."

Mr. Lawson looked embarrassed and stared down at his feet. "There's no need for that, Rachel," he said quietly.

"No, I insist! I want to show that my apology is sincere," said Rachel, handing him some bills. "I did not behave like a lady, and I'm sorry. It's taken me this amount of time to recover. That Hetty King gets under my skin more than any woman on this good earth. Before I know it, she makes me say things that I always come to regret." She straightened her shoulders. "Anyway, I've said my piece, and now I hope we can forget about the whole thing."

Mrs. Lawson smiled at her old friend. "Of course, Rachel."

Outside the general store, Theodore Simpkin and Abner Jeffries pulled up in the buggy. Abner gingerly put his hand out to clutch the basket, and the silence of the street was broken by the sudden cry of the baby. The poor thing had woken from the sleep the motion of the buggy had lulled him into, and started quite rightly to scream his lungs out.

Behind the safety of his counter, Mr. Lawson tried to change the subject. He was never comfortable in the face of someone else's apology. "Well, uh...any word about the baby yet, Rachel?" he ventured, not realizing what dangerous territory he was treading on.

"Not a word. It's in God's hands, that's what," Rachel replied piously, adjusting her bonnet.

Mrs. Potts sidled up to her and said in a cloying voice, "In many ways, it must be a relief to you."

Rachel turned on her indignantly. "Well hardly, Clara Potts! But Providence knows, if I was meant to look after that baby, it would not have disappeared as it did."

Abner and Mr. Simpkin chose that moment to enter the store, carrying the basket, crying baby and all, between them. Everyone in the store stopped and stared when the doorbell rang. Especially Rachel Lynde, who seemed clearly startled at the sight.

"What in heaven's name...?" the poor woman barely managed to utter.

"We found your baby for you, Mrs. Lynde,"

said Abner triumphantly. "As you can see, he's safe and sound."

"Now see here, Abner..." began Rachel, the expression on her face betraying her real shock and embarrassment.

Both Mrs. Lawson and Mrs. Potts rushed to look at the crying baby in the basket. Mrs. Potts turned around coyly. "Providence moves in mysterious ways, doesn't it, Rachel?" she purred.

The bell clanged again and Hetty rushed in, huffing and puffing, obviously out of breath from keeping up with the buggy.

She and Rachel stared at one another as the others stood around awkwardly, looking from the screaming baby to the two women. After a moment's silence, Rachel seized the basket right from under Hetty's nose and glared at her triumphantly. She knew full well that she couldn't possibly lose face in front of all these people.

Hetty scowled back defiantly, but it was obvious to all that she was keenly upset.

"So, Rachel Lynde, you've got what you wanted!" she spat out. Then she turned on her heel and stalked out of the store.

Chapter Twenty-Two

That night, a very quiet Abigail and Malcolm sat before their fireplace, lost in their own thoughts. Malcolm rose from his chair and added another piece of wood, the sparks shooting upwards into the chimney as he dropped it with a thump into the grate. He stirred up the coals with the poker, making sure there was plenty of air space between the logs as the flames flickered and caught. He stayed hunched down for a moment, staring into the flames.

"He was a very handsome baby, wasn't he, Abigail?" he said suddenly.

Abigail looked at his back and answered, not sure how her voice was going to come out. "Yes, yes he was." She swallowed painfully. "Please don't talk about him, Malcolm."

"I wondered..." he went on quietly. "Well, that is, what if I talked to Rachel Lynde and kind of made her see that—"

"Please Malcolm," Abigail interrupted. "I just can't bear thinking we could have him back, if it isn't meant to be." Her voice shook with suppressed emotion. Malcolm turned and looked at her, then came to sit beside her on the settee.

"Oh Abby darlin'. There now," he soothed, his arm around her. "That's an awful lot of sadness for someone who isn't 'the mothering kind.'"

Abigail let go of her tears almost in relief, and they flowed relentlessly down her face. "Oh Malcolm," she sobbed into his shirt as he gathered her to him. "You know me better than I know myself. What would I ever do without you?"

Chapter Twenty-Three

Green Gables nestled comfortably behind a row of tall apple trees that shielded it from the view of the road that ran by and into the village of Avonlea. It was always a picture of serenity, but on this particular day its walls hid a scene that was anything but calm.

Rachel Lynde, looking haggard and unkempt, scurried hither and thither in the kitchen, attempting to calm the screaming baby. She wore an old, tattered dressing gown, and her hair was held raggedly back in a braid from the night before, even though it was the middle of the afternoon. She groaned as she realized the bottles were boiling over on her stove, but just as she rushed to remove them from the heat, there was a knock at her front door.

"Oh no," she breathed. The knock was repeated, this time louder.

"All right! All right," she called, then looked around frantically for the basket. Seeing it, she raced over and placed the baby gently down into its covers. "I'm just going to put you down," she said. "There, there, ooh yes, just stay, for a little while," she cooed as she backed away from the basket. The baby, in reply, let out an unearthly scream and Rachel raced back to the basket, swooped the baby out and grabbed a bottle from the table.

"There now! Don't cry! You're just fine, sweetheart! Yes, yes, yes! We will get something for you to drink. Oh yes!" she mumbled as she headed for the door.

Rachel, the infant in her arms, ran into the hall. She reached out to put the bottle down to have a free hand to open the door, but she misjudged the distance to the hall table as she flew by, and the bottle crashed to the floor, spilling milk all over the rug. She rolled her eyes with frustration and opened the door.

To her horror, who should be standing there but Mrs. Potts. Rachel took one look and fled back into the kitchen for another bottle, which she put into the crying baby's mouth. Not waiting for an invitation, Mrs. Potts followed her, taking great note of Rachel's appearance.

"What can I do for you, Mrs. Potts?" asked Rachel, through gritted teeth.

"Rachel, I hardly recognized you," said Mrs. Potts, her voice as sweet as syrup. "I just thought I'd drop by with this sweater for Marilla to give Anne. I expected I'd see you at the sewing circle yesterday but..."

"I was unable to go," replied Rachel bluntly.

"Is there anything I can do to help?" Mrs. Potts persisted, nosing around, trying to size up the situation.

Rachel steered Mrs. Potts towards the door and talked over the baby's screaming. "Not a thing Mrs. Potts," she said, most ungraciously. "I have everything under control. Goodbye!"

A protesting Mrs. Potts found herself on the doorstep of Green Gables, the baby's cries still ringing in her ears. She squared her shoulders, arched an eyebrow and, armed with all her news, marched purposefully down the road in the direction of Avonlea.

"I'm telling you the absolute truth! Rachel Lynde is breaking under the strain! She looked like an unmade bed. Her hair was hanging down her back like a cat's tail!" Mrs. Potts exclaimed, as if these facts alone formed the absolute and unquestionable proof of Rachel's inability to cope. The woman was having the time of her life, holding court around the potbellied stove in the general store.

"Rachel would rather die than let anyone see her in that state," said an incredulous Mrs. Lawson, who had listened avidly to all Mrs. Potts had to say.

Hetty King went about her business in the background, pretending not to give a hoot about the predicament Rachel Lynde found herself in. "Well, if you ask me, that baby would be better off in an orphanage than with her," she couldn't help but comment, despite the disinterested look she had planted on her face.

Mrs. Potts looked at Mrs. Lawson with her eyebrows raised knowingly. "You surprise me, Hetty King. I always thought you had more gumption."

Hetty pursed her lips and buried her head in the pattern book, ostensibly looking for a suitable pinafore for Sara.

Mrs. Potts pursued her theme. "How can you just stand there? If I was you, I'd be on Rachel's doorstep. It's plain as plain she can't keep up with that child."

"And you're the one who spoke for it in the first place!" added Mrs. Lawson.

Hetty turned and faced them both. "I wouldn't set foot in Green Gables if it were the last shelter on earth!"

Chapter Twenty-Four

And so it was that Hetty King found herself snooping around Green Gables that very afternoon. She stealthily approached the back door, telling herself that she would just peek through one of the windows to assure herself that the baby was fine and then she would leave. No sooner had she leaned down and screwed up one eye—the better to see through the window—when the kitchen screen door slammed open and out came Rachel Lynde, still looking like the wrath of God and twice as angry.

"How dare you come poking your nose around here, Hetty King?" she hissed. "You haven't come calling on me in thirty-odd years. Why bother now?"

Momentarily caught off guard, Hetty recovered herself quickly and decided that the best defense was an offense. "I'm here because I have a bone to pick with you, Rachel Lynde!" she stated coldly and clearly. "Oh," she smiled coyly, "I've heard all the stories in town! But then you never fooled me! You didn't really want this baby at all, did you? And now you've got it, you can't take care of it!"

Rachel narrowed her eyes at Hetty and then closed the door behind her with great indignation. "Don't raise your voice so. I've just got that baby to sleep! Please, just mind your own business and leave."

Hetty stood her ground, her hands on her hips. "I will not leave until I've seen the child is safe and sound."

"That child is perfectly fine in every respect," said Rachel, nose to nose with Hetty, daring her to doubt her word.

"I won't leave until I see it!" stated Hetty, stubbornly.

Rachel sighed, realizing that she wasn't going to rid herself of Hetty so easily. "Oh for heaven's sake!" she exclaimed, turning her back on Hetty to open the door.

She tried to turn the knob—first one way, and then the other. Hetty attempted to look over her shoulder, wondering why on earth it was taking the woman so long to open a door. Rachel shifted to block her view. She grabbed the knob again and yanked on the door with all her might, but it wouldn't budge.

"Look what you've done!" She turned to Hetty in furious exasperation.

"What I've done!" Hetty exploded. She pushed in front of Rachel to try the door herself. "You're the one who was foolish enough to lock yourself out." Then the realization dawned on both of them at the same time. "And Jane's baby is alone in there!" accused Hetty.

Rachel's face went white, and not just with the cold she was beginning to feel through the thin material of her dress. "One of the windows must be open!" she said, frantically fumbling with the latches on the windows that lined the porch. They were all locked securely. She ran down the steps and looked up at an open window above the porch roof. "Now I'll have to go in through the bedroom." She looked at Hetty with a scowl on her face. "Gracious Providence, Hetty King, you are nothing but trouble! That's what!"

She stormed around the corner of the house and reappeared carrying a ladder. She clumsily propped it against the porch roof, huffing and puffing. Beads of sweat began to form on her red face, despite the chill in the air. She gathered up her voluminous skirts and, putting one foot gingerly on the bottom rung, she balanced her great weight on it and attempted to climb. There was a sharp cracking sound, and the wooden rung gave way.

"Well, I suppose you'll be needing some help, will you, Rachel?" commented Hetty with sarcasm.

"Not from you, Hetty King," fumed Rachel. "I'd never take anything from you."

"You took Romney Penhallow's heart away from me, Rachel!"

"Oh, don't harp on him again, Hetty," replied Rachel impatiently, more absorbed in finding a secure spot to lean the ladder than listening. "You have been sadly mistaken all these years, you know, if you think I wilfully stole him away from you."

Hetty looked up at the window that Rachel intended to enter, and then at Rachel's ample hips. It would be like fitting a square peg into a round hole. "You'll never fit through that!" she exclaimed.

Rachel's face turned redder than ever.

"Here," Hetty continued, motioning Rachel away from the ladder before the woman could think of a retort, "I'll get in the blasted window!"

Hetty tested the second rung and then pulled herself up, taking step after step until she reached the roof of the porch.

Rachel watched her from below, holding onto the ladder with both hands. "Careful," she cautioned as Hetty scrambled onto the roof on her hands and knees.

"Just you hang on down there, that's all," snapped Hetty from her perch.

"I never even wanted to go out with him," said Rachel.

"With who? Whom?" Hetty called down, puffing with exertion. She had momentarily forgotten what she and Rachel had been discussing, so involved had she been in the process of getting her legs from the top rung of the ladder to the roof in a somewhat ladylike manner.

"Romney," shouted Rachel. "I only did it because I was jealous."

Hetty peered down at her from the roof. "Jealous! Jealous of what?"

"You had that new ermine muff." Rachel looked off into the distance, as if she could still see it.

"What? What ermine muff?" Hetty frowned, not comprehending what Rachel was talking about.

"The one with the bells that hung down. You got it for Christmas, and I wanted one just like it, but my mother said it was too ostentatious."

"Ermine muff?" repeated Hetty, trying desperately to remember. She crawled very carefully, on her hands and knees, across the roof to the window, and then pushed the window sash up as far as it would go.

"The one that Romney stepped on when we were at the Sloanes' skating party," called Rachel, straining to see where Hetty had got to.

"It wasn't ermine. It was beaver," replied Hetty, suddenly recalling the incident. "He absolutely ruined it, didn't he?"

"He was a clumsy fool of a boy," shouted Rachel. "I never understood why you liked him. He had such dreadful teeth. And no chin!"

Hetty smiled at the memory. "That's right," she chuckled. "He really didn't have a chin, did he?" She started to laugh quietly to herself as she pushed through the narrow opening of the window, her sticklike legs waving in the air as she entered the upstairs bedroom head first.

Hetty was still chuckling as she made her way down the stairs and into the front hall of Green Gables. "Romney Penhallow," she said to herself, shaking her head, and as she let Rachel in the front door, a new wave of mirth overtook her. "And do you remember how all the other boys called him 'owl-eyes'?"

Rachel let out a snort. "It was because of those glasses he wore!" She and Hetty started to laugh so hard that tears came to their eyes and they had to sit down on the stairs.

"He was balding at eleven," Rachel managed to say before she was convulsed once again with the hilarity of it all.

Hetty laughed hysterically, clutching her side and gripping Rachel's arm. Then she stopped short, realizing they were supposed to be mortal enemies. She paused and looked at the woman sitting next to her, remembering her as she had been when they were best friends all the way through school. Until grade seven, that is. She hesitated and cleared her throat. "I have to admit, Rachel," she began slowly. "Perhaps we've both been somewhat foolish all these years."

Rachel wiped her eyes and stared at Hetty. "Well, I've always been one to let bygones be bygones, Hetty. It was you who insisted on quarreling."

"Me?" protested Hetty sharply. But before Rachel's comment could start another thirty-year war, Jane Morris's baby started screaming from the kitchen.

Rachel dragged her great bulk from the bottom of the stairs. "There, you see what you've done? You've woken him! Now I'll have no peace for the rest of the day!" She raced towards the kitchen, but the more agile Hetty cut in front of her.

Hetty reached the basket on the kitchen table first and picked up its loudly crying contents. "Hush hush, young man! Don't carry on so!" she soothed, bouncing the baby up and down in front of her. The baby twisted and squirmed. "Now, now! Be quiet!" Hetty requested. "No, no, don't wriggle so!"

Rachel stepped in with authority. "Give him to me, Hetty! I'll settle him!" and she took the baby from a protesting Hetty. The baby, not at all pleased at being moved around so much so soon after waking, screamed all the more.

"Oh yes. You've settled him all right, haven't you?" said Hetty, cackling sarcastically.

Rachel had finally reached a state that was beyond pretense. She looked at Hetty in desperation, her hair sticking to a face shining with perspiration. "This is the way it has been for the past forty-eight hours, Hetty. I have been at my wits' end, I don't mind saying. If Marilla comes home to this, I won't have a home to call my own!"

"Now calm yourself, Rachel," said Hetty, taking charge of the situation. "The child is all frazzled because the two of us are in such a tizzy. I know from my teaching experience never to let a child know what you're really feeling."

At that moment, there was a knock on the door, and Rachel looked, wild-eyed, towards it.

"Why is it that when you don't want company, there is a never-ending stream arriving at your door?" She handed the baby over to a surprised Hetty and raced out of the room.

Hetty beamed at the infant, pleased to have him to herself, but he took one look at her and screamed even louder. A desperate look came into Hetty's eyes as she bounced him up and down, singing, "Ring around the rosy, A pocket full of posies..."

Rachel opened the front door to see Malcolm MacEwan, of all people, standing there, his arms full of wrapped packages and toys, his buggy tied to the Green Gables fence.

Rachel for once was seemingly without words, so Malcolm began the conversation.

"Pardon me for intruding on your quiet, Mrs. Lynde, but I couldn't resist stopping by. Abby and I became quite fond of the wee fellow. May I come in? I've brought a few things for him." The sound of the baby screaming was highly audible from the kitchen. "Oh, I can hear him all right. Good pair of lungs," commented Malcolm cheerfully as he made his way past a stunned Rachel in the direction of the cry.

"Is there any point in asking you to sit down?" asked Rachel sarcastically, finally finding her voice and following in his wake.

Hetty looked quite comical, bouncing from foot to foot, humming nursery rhymes and trying to calm the baby, as Malcolm entered the kitchen.

"Hello there, Lucky!" he grinned as he took the baby from a relieved Hetty.

"Lucky! What kind of name is that?" she muttered in surprise.

Rachel followed him in, and looked at him disdainfully. "And what, may I ask, do you know about babies, Malcolm MacEwan?"

"Nothing. Nothing at all!" replied Malcolm as he slung the baby over his shoulder and patted his back. "Atta boy! There's a fellow. It's all right now, you're safe and sound." The infant ceased crying immediately.

Hetty and Rachel glanced at each other. Malcolm then swooped the baby from his shoulder, making both women gasp in horror and race forward to catch it, certain he would fall straight to the floor. But, of course, Malcolm held him firmly and started swinging him gently in a circular motion, out and away from his body, the same movement that miners use when they are panning for gold. The baby was delighted, and chuckled and gurgled, his face all dimples and smiles.

Hetty stepped forward gingerly and playfully tickled the baby, now that he was settled. "You have a real knacky way with babies, Malcolm. No denying that."

Rachel nodded in agreement. "You're more of a mother than the two of us put together. That's what!"

Chapter Twenty-Five

The first snow of winter fell gently as the buggy pulled up in front of Abigail and Malcolm's house. The lamps in the parlor were lit, throwing rays of light onto the clean, new white flakes as they silently covered the miniature rosebushes. Malcolm jumped down from the driver's seat, his leather miner's jacket wrapped around him against the wind.

In the parlor, Sara and Felicity helped a very subdued Abigail to pack blankets and nappies into a box for Felicity to take home.

"Who knows, Felicity," said Abigail with false bravado. "Maybe your mother will have use for these again some day."

Sara and Felicity looked at each other sadly and continued to pack. Sara had never felt so defeated. She knew her aunts hoped that she had learned a great lesson from all that had come to pass, but, unfortunately, that was not the case. She would never admit it to them, but if she had it all to do over again, she would do exactly as she had done.

The sound of the front door closing interrupted her thoughts. Abigail looked up, recognizing Malcolm's footsteps. A scraping sound came from the hallway. She could hardly believe her ears. He was actually cleaning his boots off before he came into the room. She shook her head. Somehow it didn't mean that much any more. She missed the untidiness, the confusion, the clamor. The house would always be too silent for her now that the baby had gone.

Malcolm appeared in the doorway, his great coat still slung casually over his shoulders. "Hello," he greeted them all cheerily. "How is everyone?"

Sara looked at him, her big, solemn blue eyes telling him exactly how they all were.

"Goodness, where have you been?" questioned Abigail, a little put out that he had disappeared mid-afternoon without a word of explanation.

"Oh, I paid a little visit to Rachel Lynde, to see the baby," said Malcolm nonchalantly, ambling over to the fireplace.

"Oh? How is he?" asked Abigail slowly, still packing, not wanting to appear to be too concerned.

"Fine. He looked very healthy." Malcolm picked up the fire tongs and started poking at the logs in the hearth.

"And how is Rachel?" asked Abigail, sounding much more charitable than she felt.

Sara wished she could close her ears entirely. She couldn't bear listening to all of this. She wondered how Abigail could. Sara could tell just how heartbroken Abigail was, even though she was trying hard not to show it.

"She's fine," replied Malcolm pleasantly. "Hetty King was there helping her."

Sara's mouth dropped and her eyes flew open. "Aunt Hetty was helping Rachel Lynde?!" She was dumbfounded.

"Well, as I live and breathe," said Abigail, swallowing her emotions. "So, everything is working out fine then, I guess."

"As fine as fine could be," said Malcolm, beaming cheerfully, as a flame finally leapt to life in the fireplace and its warmth started to fill the room.

"You needn't be in such good humor about it, Malcolm," snapped Abigail, the edge in her voice betraying her true feelings.

Malcolm turned and stood with his back to the hearth, the portrait of Abigail's father glaring over his shoulder. "Oh now, it's not that bad, Abby. The baby is well taken care of. Come and give me a hug."

For the very first time since she had met Malcolm, Sara felt herself beginning to get angry with him. How could he be so insensitive? She thought he loved the baby. How could he dismiss it to the care of others so quickly? Especially Rachel Lynde!

Abigail looked as if she shared Sara's feelings. She stared at Malcolm stubbornly, no trace of a smile on her face. In fact, she quite resembled the Reverend Ward at that moment.

"I'm not in a hugging mood, Malcolm."

Malcolm raised his eyebrows in mock dismay

and glanced at Sara and Felicity, who were also, obviously, not in a hugging mood.

"Oh, it's come to this, has it? I can't get a hug from my wife on our one-month anniversary?"

Abigail's face softened. She took a breath and looked down at the sparkling diamond ring on her left hand. She twisted it self-consciously. "Why, so it is. Yes, you can have a hug, Mr. MacEwan." She crossed the room and allowed herself to be enfolded by his arms. She pulled back suddenly. Something was not right.

"Not too hard, Abby," said Malcolm softly. "You'll wake the wee fellow. And Lord knows, he hasn't had that much sleep in the last two days or so."

Abigail stared up at him in disbelief. His blue-black eyes twinkled wickedly as he pulled his coat off his shoulders and revealed the peacefully sleeping baby in the crook of his arm.

Abigail's eyes filled with tears and a little sob escaped her lips. "The baby!" she gasped, hardly believing her eyes. "It's the baby!"

Sara and Felicity leapt off the settee where they had been sitting glumly, and were now alternately hugging Abigail and Malcolm and trying to get a peek at the baby.

"He's home!" shouted Sara with glee.

"Are you going to keep him?" asked Felicity, coming straight to the point, asking the question Sara had been unable to voice.

"What about Rachel? What about Hetty?" stammered Abigail, trying to make sense of the situation.

"They both agreed that they'd make much better godmothers than they would parents," replied Malcolm. "On the condition, however, that they could both help out on a regular basis."

"But what about that lawyer?" insisted Abigail, hoping it wasn't all too good to be true. "It has to be legal!"

"Rachel is prepared to legalize it. And that ridiculous Simpkin fellow is probably halfway back from Charlottetown by now. I have a strong feeling he simply wants the whole affair over and done with."

Malcolm hugged Abigail with his free arm, and the tears flowed down her cheeks quite openly now. She didn't care who saw them.

"You see," said Sara smugly to Felicity, speaking without thinking. "I knew it would all work out."

Felicity raised her eyebrows warningly, and too late Sara realized that she had most likely let the cat out of the bag.

The implication was not missed by Abigail and Malcolm, who stopped gazing at the baby adoringly for one second, looked at each other and then turned their eyes upon Sara and Felicity.

"Well..." stammered Sara. "I did. I mean, we did, not just me...I..." she finished lamely.

Malcolm exchanged a knowing look with his wife. "Something tells me that there's more than meets the eye here," he said, his voice stern.

Sara and Felicity squirmed uncomfortably, guilt written all over their innocent faces.

"But," Malcolm continued gravely, "every good gold miner knows that you take your luck where you find it..." he paused. "...And you don't ask any questions." A small smile formed and his eyes had a familiar twinkle.

Sara and Felicity beamed in relief, and all four crowded around the baby, now happy in Abigail's arms, his face flushed and peaceful with sleep.

Outside the little house, the snow continued to fall softly. Autumn had said goodbye to Avonlea, and already, beneath the carpet of white, new life began to grow, with great promises of spring.

🍃   🍃   🍃